STORE-BOUGHT BABY

STORE-BOUGHT BABY

SANDRA BELTON

GREENWILLOW BOOKS
An Imprint of HarperCollinsPublishers

VERY SPECIAL THANKS TO THE FOLLOWING FOR THEIR CONTRIBUTIONS TO THE
DEVELOPMENT OF THIS BOOK: TO CLIFTON ANTHONY ROBINSON, MD, FOR HIS POEM
"PEACE BROTHER"; TO SUSAN VERNON OF THE CRADLE, IN EVANSTON, ILLINOIS,
FOR INFORMATION REGARDING ADOPTION ISSUES; TO CAROL LYNN PEARSON FOR
PERMISSION TO REPRINT EXCERPTS FROM HER POEM "MY OWN CHILD," FROM HER BOOK
BEGINNINGS; AND TO CESAREO MORENO FOR INFORMATION REGARDING THE MEXICAN
FINE ARTS CENTER MUSEUM. A BOUQUET OF THANKS TO PATRICIA ASHBY FOR
LENDING A KIND, LISTENING EAR AND SHARING A KNOWING AND LOVE OF GARDENS.

Store-Bought Baby

The text of this book is set in Adobe Garamond. Book design by Chad W. Beckerman.

Library of Congress Cataloging-in-Publication Data
Belton, Sandra.
Store-bought baby / by Sandra Belton.
p. cm.
"Greenwillow Books."
Summary: The death of Leah's beloved older brother, and her parents' reactions
to the tragedy, raise questions for Leah about the meaning of family and about
her place in her own.
ISBN-10: 0-06-085086-8 (trade bdg.) ISBN-13: 978-0-06-085086-9 (trade bdg.)
ISBN-10: 0-06-085087-6 (lib. bdg.) ISBN-13: 978-0-06-085087-6 (lib. bdg.)
[1. Grief—Fiction. 2. Death—Fiction. 3. Family—Fiction. 4. Adoption—Fiction.
5. Brother—Fiction. 6. African Americans—Fiction. 7. Chicago (Ill.)—Fiction.] I. Title.
PZ7.B4197Sto 2006 [Fic]—dc22 2005022038

First Edition 10 9 8 7 6 5 4 3 2 1

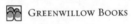 GREENWILLOW BOOKS

from what the police report said i was probably
kissing lester at the exact time
my brother killed himself
wouldn't mama just love to hear that

maybe one of these days i'll tell her
not only that but everything she needs to hear
she and dad both
i'll say mama you and dad keep saying how your son
died in an automobile accident
you need to get off that lie
and start telling the truth
he KILLED himself
HE was the one driving the car
HE was the one going too fast down that rained on slick street
HE was the one acting like a fool not slowing down
HE did the killing and then he did the dying

maybe then i'll tell her that if my brother walked through the
front door right now i'd feel like killing him all over again
myself

❧ I ❧

BIBI LOOKS UP FROM THE PICTURES SPREAD ACROSS her lap. "Leah, would you mind slipping out there to get me something to eat?"

I don't want to leave the room, even for my grandmother. But I keep that out of my voice and don't look at her when I answer. "What do you want?"

"Whatever. There's food from one end of that kitchen to the other. Just pick up a little something I can munch on."

I want her to be more specific. A piece of fruit? A slice of cake or pie? Something like a sandwich? But I don't ask Bibi anything else. I guess I'm glad she's thinking about something besides the pile of pictures she's been fingering through ever since she sat down.

Luce in a Santa hat. The picture for the Christmas card that year.

Luce with both grandmothers. Bibi and Grandma Myrtle.

Luce and me running into the ocean that first time.

Luce with Cliff at Great America.

Luce, Luce, Luce.

I close the door behind me when I leave Bibi's room. Before I even take three steps, I can see that people are still everywhere. Groups of them all over the house. Talking. Eating. Eating and talking.

"Dr. Ash's message was quite comforting, don't you think? I mean, under the circumstances."

Mrs. Lacy. Wearing that strong perfume. How can she stand it?

"That's the plant we sent. See? Over there, next to the piano."

What difference does it make, Mrs. Cass? Who really cares?

I say nothing. I keep my head down and my eyes on the floor and walk through the crowd as fast as I can. Past my room. Down the hall. Through the dining room. I'm tempted to look around just to see if Mahri came over after the services like everyone else, but I don't. I hope that not looking anywhere will keep everyone out of my face. Make it easier for me to ignore anyone calling my name.

I get to the kitchen and see that Bibi's right. Food covers every inch of counter and table space. Covered platters and casserole dishes. Cakes and pies wrapped in clear plastic. Baskets of fruit. Crates of pop and six-packs of water bottles.

Bags and boxes of chips. Cookies. Food's even stacked up in corners where there's no table or counter space. Food is everywhere just like the people.

When I stop and wonder what I can pick up quick that Bibi would want, I start feeling sick just seeing all that food. Before I can move again, a hand from someone standing in the kitchen grabs onto me.

"Leah." The hand is hot on my arm, even through my sweater. "Baby, you want me to fix you something?"

It's Mrs. Clark. The lady from the Missionary Guild who's always around after funerals to be in charge of food. She plants herself in front of me and I know I have to look at her.

"Here, let me make you a nice plate. Would you like some roast beef? We have a delicious ham, already sliced. Let's see. . . ." Mrs. Clark swoops across the food, pulling off wraps like she's uncovering a treasure. She stops in front of the biggest find of all and unrolls the foil slowly. Carefully. "Ahhhh," she breathes. "How about a nice turkey plate? This golden bird's been waiting for somebody to take a juicy bite." She pulls at a platter holding the biggest turkey I've ever seen in my life.

The sunlight slicing through the kitchen blinds makes me squint. It lands on curls pinned at the top of Mrs. Clark's head. Her wig. Reddish gold curls in the yellow light.

Suddenly the light makes me dizzy. Mixed up. I know I'm still standing there in front of her and Beast Turkey. I still hear her asking me what I want, but her voice is fading away and somehow I'm not really there with her at all.

It's impossible, I know, but I begin to see Luce where Mrs. Clark is standing. My brother. In that exact spot. The broken slices of sun coming through blinds are landing on his head, turning the tips of his silky brown curls into strands of reddish gold. I squint harder.

I remember.

It was Thanksgiving morning. Luce had come to the kitchen to help Mama. Because of their deal. If he helped fix dinner, he would be able to leave early to have dessert with Mahri. His girlfriend. At her house.

Mama told Luce to wash the turkey and pat it dry. He made a face. "Aw, Ma, not that." He pushed up against Mama. "You said there was a lot to do. Give me a job that doesn't involve this . . . this bird."

"And why on earth not?"

"Come on, Ma. You know I'm a vegetarian. Don't ask me to handle this poor dead animal." Luce reached across Mama and took the little knife and half-peeled potato out of her hands. "Here. Let me do this. Cut up the potatoes. Food for the righteous."

Mama sucked her teeth. "Boy, you and that vegetarian obsession both are getting on my nerves." She nudged Luce away from the sink with her hip and reached for the turkey. "You just make sure I don't see you anywhere near the dressing. I'm not stuffing it into the turkey, but I'm making it with turkey broth. And I'm adding sausage to one batch of dressing and oysters to the other."

Luce stood there in his pajamas and bare feet, grinning. "Better add some more potatoes to that pile, Ma." He twirled his perfect peeling curl in Mama's face. "I got a feeling my dinner plate's gonna look like a snow-covered mountain this year."

A breath's worth of silence. The sideways looks at each other. Then the bursts of laughter. High and low. The Mama and Luce routine.

I remember.

Mrs. Clark moves her head and the sunlight becomes a shadow. The sound of her voice makes my eyes open wider and I'm looking again at Beast Turkey on the counter and understand what she's saying.

"Want some turkey and dressing with gravy? Perhaps a few green beans?" She has a large carving knife in her hand and keeps talking while she raises it above the huge brown breast. "Or maybe you'd rather I make you a sandwich. . . ."

I put my hand over my mouth to keep from screaming. From telling Mrs. Clark in that stupid wig that I'm not hungry. Not even a little bit. That's what I think at first. Then I think it's there to keep me from yelling at everybody. From screaming that today, of all days, even having all that meat in the house is disgusting!

Then I know the real reason. I clamp my hand tighter over my mouth and push my way through the people stacking up in the kitchen like the food. I kick open the back door to make it outside in time.

I run down the steps and across the concrete squares where the Dumpsters are kept. I have to get to where there's grass. To throw up. Over and over. I know I haven't eaten in days and wonder where it's all coming from. The same thing I've wondered about the tears.

❧ 2 ❧

"LEAH? LEAH, BABY, ARE YOU OKAY?"

Mrs. Clark has followed me outside and is standing on our porch. But she can't see me. I'm on the other side of the big forsythia bush, leaning against the porch of the unit next to ours. The Glenns' porch. Hearing Mrs. Clark's voice, I press against the thick wooden posts.

Please leave me alone. Please. Please!

I hold my breath when she calls again.

"Leah? You out here?"

The spring of the safety latch squeaks when the door opens again. I think Mrs. Clark has gone back inside but then I hear another voice.

"Anna? Is something wrong?"

Mama!

I press back even harder.

"Mrs. Clair?" Mrs. Clark is surprised. "Oh no, nothing's wrong. I was just . . . ah, just wondering where Leah went.

She left the kitchen in kind of a hurry and I . . . you know, I was just wondering."

"Oh." Mama's voice is little. Flat.

You're wondering, too, aren't you, Mama? Wondering like you always do about what I'm doing. If it's something I'm not supposed to be doing.

My stomach starts burning again and it feels like I'm about to gag. I automatically put my hand over my mouth. The cruddy feel of my mouth and smell of my breath make me want to jerk my hand away, but I don't.

"She probably went around to the front, Mrs. Clair. Yes, that's what she did. Don't you worry. She's all right. Leah'll be okay."

What do you know? Why don't you just shut up?

I'm pressing against the post so hard I wonder if it might bend.

"Come on back inside, Mrs. Clair. Let me fix you a plate."

I wait to hear another squeak before I let out the breath I'm holding. I wait another minute before I decide it's safe to move.

I look up and down the squares and rectangles of grass that line the long fence separating our condo complex from the alley. There doesn't seem to be anybody out in the train of backyards but me. No Levy kids in the yellow and red plastic playhouse under their porch.

Luce helped Mr. Levy put that house together.

No Mrs. O'Conner poking through the smelly compost pile in the last yard. No Mr. Jacobs on his second-floor porch, looking up and down the alley for suspicious characters.

"Stop complaining about Mr. Jacobs, Ma. He's the neighborhood watch dog. That dude's better than an alarm system!"

I close my eyes and shake my head. Again and again. Then I think how stupid I must look and stop.

I know I have to go back inside. At least to tell Bibi something about why I haven't brought her anything yet to munch on. But there's no way I'm going back in that kitchen. No way.

I decide to go around the side of the building and go inside through the front. I won't even have to ring the bell. Somebody'll be there to let me in. There's been somebody by the door ever since we came from . . . Somebody has been there all day.

I walk through the space between our building and the one next to it, staying on the narrow sidewalk that cuts through the thick ivy that grows like crazy on either side. I don't look up at the windows of our apartment, but I can tell automatically what I'm passing.

The den . . . the dining room . . . Luce's room . . .

When I get to the end of the walkway, I can hear people in front of our entrance. I stop by the gate and wait a minute before I push it open.

Get ready.

I put my head down like before and keep it that way while I pass by everyone without saying anything to anybody.

I make it through the foyer and to my parents' bedroom without running into anybody toxic. Like Mrs. Clark. Mama, Dad. I head straight for their small bathroom to wash my face and gargle. I have my hand on the door, getting ready to shut it when I hear footsteps coming into the bedroom.

Almost without realizing what I'm doing, I move to the bathtub and step into it. Shoes and all. I back up as far as I can and pull the shower curtain all the way closed, being as quiet as possible with every move. Then I freeze.

The footsteps stop just outside the bathroom door. I begin to think I'm going to be safe when I hear the voice.

"Hold on, Lou. I'm going to leave with you. I just want to freshen up my face a little bit."

I recognize the voice right away. It's heavy and raspy. A not-so-pretty voice you don't forget.

Pictures flash in my mind. Willa Vernon running into Luce and me on the street that time in front of the dojo where Luce took karate, and staring. Seeing us at one of Dad's concerts, and staring. Smiling at us over Mama's shoulder while she was hugging Mama and *pretending* to be her great friend. And staring.

You cow! That's probably why you were always staring. Always thinking about Luce being adopted. You stupid cow!

I grab the handle of the soap dish. I think I'm using it to keep from falling. From pitching over headfirst into the tub. Then I decide I'm holding on to it to keep from jumping out of the tub altogether and choking Willa Vernon totally to death.

You are worse than stupid. You're evil! Nobody in this house ever *made a deal about Luce being adopted. Especially not Mama or Dad. Luce's* real *parents.*

It feels like the words are screaming in my head. I can hardly stand hearing them and the voices in the bedroom.

"That's not fair, Willa. Luce was their son. In every sense of the word, he was their child."

Their best *child.*

Mrs. Jones's voice is getting farther away. Probably she's walking to the doorway leading into the hall.

Getting away from that cow!

"I know, Lou, but still . . ."

I stand straight up in the tub and smash my hands over my ears. I can't listen to any more. I can't.

I want to stay in the tub longer. To make certain they won't see me. But the burning starts again and I know I can't.

I climb out of the tub and make it over to the toilet just in time. But when I hang my head over the open hole, the only thing that falls onto the blue water are hot, angry tears.

🦕 3 🦕

GRANDMA MYRTLE AND AUNT MONIQUE ARE THE last ones to leave. They're going back to their hotel, even though I thought I had convinced them to stay here like they did last night. It's better when they're around. Especially Aunt Monique. I never would have gotten through last night without her. When I asked her why she wasn't staying tonight, she said she thought the family needed to have some time alone.

"You're family, Aunt Monique. Remember?"

"Most definitely, baby." She gave me one of her sweet-smelling hugs. "But you know what I mean."

Yeah. The nuclear family. The one that might bomb at any minute.

Thinking Aunt Monique has changed her mind is why I'm about to run to the door when the doorbell rings a few minutes after she and Grandma Myrtle have left. But Dad gets to the door first, opens it, and goes to the outside hall.

He probably wants to see who it is before he buzzes them in. I stop in the hallway and wait.

"Hill. Kevin." Dad's voice is surprised.

It's two of Luce's friends, all the way from when Hill and Luce met in preschool.

"Hey, Mr. Clair. I hope it's okay for us to be stopping by. You see, we wanted . . ." Hill's voice from the outside hall is deeper than I remember.

"No, no. This is fine. Come on in."

Dad backs through the door into our foyer. I step backward, down the way I came. Into the deep shadow the light makes at the bend of our hallway. The spot I used to be scared to walk through after dark when I was little.

Kevin is Hill's little brother. Except neither of them is anywhere close to little now. Hill is over six two and Kevin is even taller. I used to think that Hill was beyond fine, but watching the two of them walk into our foyer it crosses my mind that Kevin might be even cuter. A second later another picture automatically slips into my mind.

Hill and Kevin stopping by to pick up Luce. The three of them standing in the foyer laughing with Mama and Dad and promising to drive carefully and keep the curfew. The three of them totally awesome together.

I shut my eyes and push farther into the shadow.

"Hill. Kevin." Mama comes out into the foyer from the living room where she and Dad had been, saying the same thing he said. In a flat "I'm surprised" voice.

"Hey, Mrs. Clair. Like I was saying to your husband, we didn't want to disturb you or anything, but we wanted you to know about this before the day was over. I mean, we were at the services and everything, but we didn't get a chance to see you after and we felt that this might be the best time to . . ."

While I'm standing there listening to Hill, my mind just takes over. I can't keep it from going to other places. Other times.

Luce and Hill chasing me up and down our long hall with light sabers, calling me calling me Princess Leia even though I kept yelling that I was R2-D2. . . .

Luce and Hill practicing their break-dancing moves and making me promise not to tell Mama that they were the ones who accidentally chipped the wood on the kitchen table. . . .

Luce and Hill hiding in the guest bathroom and taking turns jumping out to scare me and whoever else they hear coming down the hall.

The other times and places are so clear in my mind, I can't hold back the hot new tears that start running down my face. I lay against the safe wall of my shadow place while the voices in the foyer keep going.

"Won't you come on in and sit down, Hill? Kevin?" I can tell that Mama's trying hard to sound more than just polite.

"Oh, no thanks, Mrs. Clair. We don't want to . . . we shouldn't stay." Kevin's voice is almost as deep as Hill's. "We just wanted you to know what we have for Luce."

For Luce?

My head jerks away from the wall. I'm thinking that Mama's and Dad's heads probably jerk a little, too.

Hill rushes to explain what his brother means. "In memory of Luce. We have something in his memory."

I try not to make a sound as I move away from the wall to look around the bend. I want to see what Hill and Kevin have, but I don't see anything.

"We have a tree. Do you want to see it?"

I'm not surprised to hear the quiet after Kevin's announcement. I know *I* sure wouldn't know what to say if I were standing there.

A tree? Where?

It's like Hill's plugged into my mind. "We bought a tree to plant in Luce's memory. We left it outside. That's why we thought you might . . ."

He sounds embarrassed.

Hill talks faster. "We already checked with your condominium association to see if it would be okay. You know, what kind of tree would be okay to get. Everything like that."

Kevin jumps back in. "Yeah, and somebody who works here is going to take care of planting it."

"And that's what's outside. The tree that's going to be planted."

"Yeah. In Luce's memory."

I can imagine Dad's and Mama's heads going up and down like mine is now, listening to Hill and Kevin. But I can't imagine what they're going to say.

How do you thank someone for a tree?

"That's a wonderful thought, boys. A very thoughtful gesture." Mama sounds sincere.

"Yes, fellows. Thank you. We really appreciate that. Ah, do you think we can see the tree from the windows over there?"

"Probably so."

The four of them move into the living room to look out the windows of the little bay area we call the sunroom. I hear them talking, but can't make out what they are saying.

It doesn't matter.

I decide this will be a good time to go down the rest of

the hall. But before I get very far, I hear them heading back through the living room. I push myself against the wall and freeze. I can hear them loud and clear when they reach the foyer.

"And you'll come by soon, right?"

"Yes, ma'am. We have to make sure everything gets done, you know, planted like it's supposed to be. And of course we want to put up the . . . ah, the plaque we're going to order. It'll have Luce's name and, ah . . . you know. . . ."

"We know." Dad's voice sounds so tired. "It's a fine plan, fellows. Fine."

I imagine the hand shaking and hugging that's going on in the foyer and think I should keep on to my room.

I've been trying to sleep but can't even make my eyes stay closed. Much less make my mind stay still. The quiet in the apartment helps me decide it's a good time to go to the living room to see the tree for myself.

My terry slippers don't make any noise as I move down the hall. That's why Mama and Dad don't hear me even when I'm almost right at the entrance of the living room. But I hear them and stop.

"Luce had good friends."

"Yes, he did."

They're probably sitting on the couch.

It's like I've frozen again. Only this time I really don't want to stay there. I don't want to listen. To hear my parents talking to each other in private. But I can't seem to move. I want to run back down the hall as fast as I can, but all my terry-covered feet can do is take little steps backward. Into the shadows of the foyer.

"Arranging to have that tree planted was extremely kind."

"Yes. Extremely."

Mama sounds almost too tired even to repeat what Dad is saying, which is all she's doing.

"And that poem . . . the one Cliff wrote and read at the . . . it was . . . It just sits there. At the front of my mind."

"Yes. It was magnificent." Mama makes a strange little sound. It sounds almost like a chuckle, but I know it isn't. "Our young Cliff is now a gifted young man."

"It's so easy to picture the two of them." Dad's strange little sound is more like a real chuckle. "Remember? There they'd be, sitting together all through the daylight hours at the dining room table, playing that fantasy game. Finding time to run off some energy only after it got dark."

"Ummm."

"Let's see. How did he put it in the poem? 'At night we chased fireflies, flickering phantoms in the moonlight. But

❀ 23 ❀

sometimes we sat in silence, swallowing the liquid dark. . . .'"

Yeah, that was *what Cliff wrote.*

I stand there wondering if Dad remembered the entire poem so perfectly. I can only remember the first few lines. And only part of them.

"We swam together as sharks . . . elbows angled up at our hips like fictional fins. . . ."

Dad starts talking again.

"How do we get through it, Lexie? How do we wake up for the next twenty thousand mornings knowing that we're not going to be able to see our sweet boy's face . . . not ever again . . . ?"

Dad sounds like he's choking. The sniffing sounds get so loud, I imagine it's *me* having trouble breathing. Then I feel the wetness on my gown where more tears have fallen and know that I am.

Leave. Leave!

This time I don't have any trouble moving back down the hall. From admitting to myself that everything about this horrible, hideous, most awful day of my life keeps filling me up even while it keeps spilling out. By the time I get back to my room, I'm not only mad forever with my brother, I'm jealous because I'm not just like he is: gone forever from this lousy world.

if i were a tree everybody would have to see me
i wouldn't be able to hide in shadows
or sneak around anywhere
even if i wanted to

if i were a tree
nothing would hurt me
nothing ignorant evil dumb stupid EVIL people say

i'd stand straight and strong through anything
rain wind blizzard snow
i could look everything right in the face
not be afraid of anybody knowing that i knew what they
might not want me to hear or know

there'd be other trees around
we'd all be alike
and not have to feel alone

maybe i'd stand for longer than 20,000 days
that's only 55 years

but maybe not

✤ 4 ✤

MAMA TELLS BIBI IT'S TOO COLD TO GO FOR A WALK.
"I almost froze when I went out." Mama's talking from the
bathroom where she's putting away whatever she got at the
drugstore, but her voice sounds even farther away. "That
sun'll fool you. It's bright, but it hasn't warmed up the air
all that much."

Bibi buttons up her sweater and slides her poncho over
her head. "I'll be fine, Lexie. The cool air will feel good."

Mama comes to Bibi's door. "It's more than cool, Mama,
and when the wind blows—"

"I want some air, Lexie. I *need* to get some air." Bibi keeps
pulling together the ends of the cord strung through the
top of her poncho.

I stay on Bibi's bed where I've been sitting, watching. Bibi
walks over to my mother. "Alexis, stop worrying so much."
She tugs at Mama's forehead to smooth out the wrinkles.
"It's just a short walk."

I look at Mama, waiting for her to look over at me, but her sad eyes stay on Bibi while her mouth tries to smile.

"Okay, Mama. Take your walk. Is that poncho going to be enough?"

"Quite enough. This is good wool."

I turn away. I'm so tired of seeing Mama's face, from hearing her one-note voice even when she's smiling. Plain tired.

I need to get some air, too.

"Wait up, Bibi." I get up from the bed and go past the two of them in the doorway. "I have to get my jacket. I'm going with you."

It's like Mama said. Cold outside. Especially for almost May. Even for Chicago. But the sky is bright like summer.

Summer . . .

I think about school being out before too long and wonder why I should bother going back. Why I shouldn't just stay out for the rest of the year like I have for the past few weeks. Not go back until September.

It would be so much easier then.

Bibi locks her arm in mine while we walk, setting a rhythm I have to follow. Even as cold as it is, I hope she's headed to the path by the lake. I don't make any suggestions and know after we make a couple of turns that she's not going on the lake path. She's on her way to the Perennial Garden in the park.

Bibi picks up the rhythm as we get close to the next corner. "What do you say we check out the garden, hmmm?"

I wonder if Bibi really thinks I haven't figured out where she's heading, but I don't say anything.

"I love seeing the changes from week to week—new blooms all the time. Even before the weather warms up. Why, the last time I was here . . ." Bibi's voice drifts away. I know she's remembering about the last time she walked to the garden.

Before Luce killed himself!

I feel Bibi's arm tighten against mine when we stop at the corner to wait for the light.

Perennial Garden is planted right in the middle of things, bordered on two sides by busy streets. One leads to Lake Shore Drive and always has heavy traffic; the other connects to streets leading to the university and, depending on the time of day, can also be loaded with traffic.

In a way it's bizarre to think that anybody would choose this spot for a big garden. One minute the city is everywhere. Especially the noises. Then you cross over an island that connects the two busy streets and it's like somebody has said, "Abracadabra, City, vanish! Hush now and be still."

Perennial Garden comes on you like a burst of country rising from concrete. Circles of green with rows and patches of color surround you. It's so quiet and peaceful. The only moving things are butterflies. It's a place where the city almost disappears and you can feel glad to have a little break.

Bibi's garden.

"They should name this garden after you," I said to Bibi once when we walked there. "You keep track of this place more than anybody."

Bibi chuckled. She loves flowers. I know she wishes our backyard was more than a small, shady triangle patch. Then she could make a real garden instead of just having those same clumps of flowers she plants every spring.

Clumps of flowers . . .

"Impatiens. That's what they are, Luce. Impatiens!" She would explain this same thing to Luce every year, but it didn't matter.

"Give it up, Bibi," he'd tease. "Don't spend up your energy on that tired clump of flowers. I get *impatient* just watching you waste your time."

Even loving gardens and flowers—*any* kind—as much as she does, Bibi would always laugh.

✿　✿　✿

Like she does every time we come here, Bibi tries to get me to understand about flowers. Perennials. How the impatiens she plants aren't perennials while just about all the flowers in this garden are. Like always, I mostly only half listen, but some of the flower names catch in my mind.

Monkshood. Foxglove. Corabell. Pincushion.

Daylily.

I must have said that name out loud because Bibi starts explaining how "daylily" is from a Greek word that means "beauty" and "day." She bends close to a tall stem that has lots of buds but only one opened yellow flower. "I especially like the idea of the daylily. Only one flower on a stem opens each day and it lasts just that day."

I like the idea of the daylily, too, but I don't say anything while Bibi checks out some of the other daylily stems. "This daylily clump will have orange flowers and that clump over there will have purple ones. . . ."

I wonder if she realizes she's using Luce's word to describe the flowers. Then when Bibi looks up from the stem, I think from seeing her face that maybe she's thinking the same thing I am. I don't want to ask.

Bibi keeps on about the perennials. How they come back year after year after you plant them. How they don't die at the end of the season like her impatiens do.

I hear Bibi's voice while I'm looking at the garden stretching out around us. The plants still with mostly green parts but blooms popping out here and there. These great perennials that died at the end of last summer and now will be coming back in all their glory. This year and next year and the next . . .

Stupid, stupid plants! Why do you get a chance to keep coming back?

I want to run through the whole entire garden and stomp on every plant until every single one of them is dead. As dead as dead can be. I want to do it so bad I don't realize that I've almost started until I feel Bibi's hand on my arm, holding me.

"Leah. Leah, baby." She snatches me into her arms. Bibi. My grandmother who looks a lot younger than she really is, even when she complains how the X-rays of her arthritic knees tell the truth about her age louder than she ever could. She grabs me into her arms like she's my age.

Just don't tell me that everything's gonna be okay. Please, just don't tell me that.

Bibi doesn't tell me anything. She just stands there in her precious garden, holding me tight in her arms. Forcing me to keep on crying. And crying.

For the billionth time I wish I could have at least one more minute with Luce. But I still don't know if I would try to choke him or squeeze him in a never-let-go hug.

5

DAD HAS THE TELEVISION TURNED UP SO LOUD, NONE of us hear Mama calling. At least I didn't. I don't think Dad or Bibi did either. When we see Mama standing there at the doorway of the den, Dad yells above the noise. "Lexie? Is something wrong?"

"Only that I've been calling you all to dinner." Mama's voice is angry like her face.

"Sorry, Lexie. I didn't hear you. I guess I was . . . wrapped up in the news."

You weren't even paying attention, Dad. You were just sitting there in the noise.

"Dinner's ready." Mama turns and walks away after she makes her announcement. Dad gives me and Bibi one of those "we'd better get going" looks and gets up from his chair. Bibi kind of smiles, shaking her head. I get up and follow both of them out the door.

It's normal and totally strange at the same time to be

heading to the dining room for dinner. We haven't sat down to eat together since . . . since that day. Whenever any of us feels like eating something, we just go get it. The refrigerator is still stuffed with food. At least I think it is. The only thing I've felt like eating is cold cereal, so the only thing I look in the refrigerator for is milk. And I go into the kitchen to have it only when nobody else is there.

I guess Mama decided our way of eating isn't civilized enough. Like she's *always* deciding what's right and not right for everybody in her universe. Maybe that's why she's set the table the way she has. I notice it the minute I walk into the dining room. The fake flowers from the storage closet are in the middle of the brass circle of candles she keeps on the table as decoration. Cloth napkins are at each place. All the food is in serving dishes. Even the sauce for the spaghetti. When Dad cooks sauce or soup or stew or anything like that, he always leaves it on the stove so it can stay hot. "Just serve yourself. Going straight to the pot is a good way to check out the cook while you're making sure your food is hot!" He'll say that even to company.

Not Mama, though. She always wants everything to look just so. Like putting out glasses with stems for the water and the wine she and Dad will have. There's an extra stem glass at Bibi's place, too. Bibi says wine usually gives her a headache, but sometimes she'll have a little. Like on special occasions.

So what's this occasion, Mama? A family dinner without Luce?

Dad goes to his place and stands there. "Ummm. Looks like something good."

Who you trying to fool, Dad? All your cheer is just like those flowers. Fake.

The rest of us stand at our places like Dad has. I look down at my plate to keep from looking at the empty place across from me and keep them there while Bibi says the blessing. Then we all sit down and start passing around the food Mama's cooked. Or tried to. The salad that's been tossed with a too-oily dressing. Spaghetti that's so stuck together it's almost lumpy. Marinara sauce that's probably cold by now.

I'm not hungry at all but know I have to eat something. Or act like I am so I won't have to listen to Mama go on and on.

Since she was determined to have a family dinner, I wonder why Mama didn't just use some of the never-ending leftovers. Or ask Dad to do the cooking like he does most of the time. Except for a special occasion like Thanksgiving when she wants things to be fancier than she thinks Dad would make them. But fancy isn't always good, and no mat-ter what Dad cooks, it's usually delicious.

Luce's cooking was usually delicious, too.

I put a little bit of everything on my dinner plate. Even the salad Mama put out little bowls for. I force myself to slide pieces of food onto my fork and into my mouth, but mostly I use my fork to move around shiny pieces of lettuce and cucumber on my plate. Helping them escape from the watery red line leaking from my little hill of spaghetti and sauce. It keeps me occupied and from concentrating on the empty space.

Luce's place.

But it's too hard to keep from remembering.

Luce rushed into the kitchen with a bag of groceries at eight o'clock that night, apologizing to everyone for being so late. It was after ten when all of us finally sat down to eat.

It was the summer after his sophomore year.

Last summer.

Luce had informed Mama that learning how to cook was going to be one of his summer projects. "It's time for me to take my place among all the great chefs of the world—men!"

Mama turned up her nose and looked over her glasses at Luce. "If that's the case, I suggest you sharpen your culinary skills with your father and stop bothering me."

"Ah yes, fair Mother, but you have the best recipe books!"

Luce and Mama. Laughing with their heads together, looking through Mama's collection of cookbooks that line the second shelf of the pantry cabinet.

For that first meal Luce made a recipe called "Judge's Artichoke Fettuccine." Except he didn't exactly follow the recipe. He used linguini instead of fettuccine and added cheese even though the recipe didn't say to. He mixed everything in a skillet on top of the stove instead of in a cool bowl like it said to do, *plus* he used one of Mama's fancy skillets that she keeps shiny more than cooks in. She almost passed out when she saw how the cheese had stuck to it.

But the judge's dish was delicious. The entire dinner was. Luce added apples and walnuts to the tomato and lettuce salad he tossed with Italian dressing, and even that was good.

Everybody sat around the table, laughing and talking. Especially Mama and Luce. They were the champion talkers at every meal. Getting into each other's faces and trying to trip each other up with their real and made-up facts.

"Feel free to jump in anytime, Dad, " Luce had said when he and Mama got started on music, debating whether history would remember Ray Charles longer than Bach.

"I'm enjoying the feast of just listening to you two."

"Dad! You mean my culinary delights have left you wanting?" Luce pretended he was insulted.

"To tell the truth, son, I'm stuffing myself with everything—the food *and* conversation. I can almost feel the pounds rolling on!"

All of us stuffed ourselves. Even Bibi, who said how eating that late would probably keep her up the rest of the night. "I guess it doesn't matter, though, because it's already after midnight."

We finished everything. "Heck, nothing left for my breakfast," Dad complained. Having dinner leftovers is his favorite breakfast.

Luce's midnight dinner.

Remembering. It hurts so much I want to slam my fist into my plate, scatter the cold, greasy food across the table. Then tell Mama she should never cook again. That it's stupid to eat in this room again. That maybe we should even think about moving to someplace brand-new. A house without any memories at all.

I don't slam my fist into my plate. I just look around the table through the corners of my eyes. Everybody's busy eating. Or pretending to. Nobody's looking at anybody else. There're no yellow flames from the candles nobody bothered to light to dance on the empty crystal wineglasses Dad didn't think about filling. Nobody's talking. There're only the voices from the still-turned-up-too-loud TV. The world news.

"Tanks and gunships pounded militia positions near two shrines in the center of Karbala today . . . over eighteen rebel fighters, including two Iranian clerics, are among the dead. . . . Fighting was also heavy in Najaf and neighboring Kufa, which is south of Baghdad. . . ."

I wonder if anybody's listening besides me.

"A spokesman reported by telephone from the Ugandan district of Gulu that the rebels of the eighteen-year insurgency hacked and burned to death over twenty-five people, including eight children. . . ."

Out of the corner of my eye I can see Dad shaking his head. He's listening like I am and thinking how terrible the news is.

I try to shut out the sound of the TV and concentrate on the *clink-clink* of silverware hitting against the plates as we all keep playing the eating game. But pieces of the news still slip through. After a while I start wondering what I feel sorriest about—what seems to be the absolute worst that is happening. Then I look across the table from me, and don't wonder anymore. I know.

❧ 6 ❧

I DON'T LOOK AT THE CLOCK BUT I CAN FEEL THAT IT'S early. One of the baby hours.

Baby hours . . .

I think at first that maybe I'm not really awake. That I'm still night dreaming. Then I know it's the sound of the rain and the spell of the dark that makes me feel it. Almost hear it.

Luce's voice.

Even though I know it's only in my head, the memory of that night falls over me like it was a blanket on my bed.

It had been storming that night, too—thundering and lightning along with the rain. The sounds woke me up into a room that was totally dark. My night-light was out. So were the lights I was used to seeing under my door and outside my window.

I was so scared it felt like I could hear the thumping of my heart. It was beating so hard and fast I knew I would be able to see it hitting against my pajamas. I looked down at my chest but it was too dark to make anything out. And that's when I had heard the voice.

"*Tika-Tika. Don't be afraid, Tika-Tika. . . .*"

It was Luce opening my door while he tapped on it and calling my name over and over while he walked into my room.

"*Tika, Tika-Tika. . . .*"

I knew who it was but kept holding my breath and listening to make sure.

Luce kept talking while he walked closer to the bed. "Don't be scared, Tika. Especially not now. It's one of the baby hours."

Even as scared as I was, I automatically knew I had to stop my brother from making fun of me. "I'm *not* scared, and stop calling me a baby."

Luce sat down next to my legs. "I would never call you a baby, Tika. You're almost six."

"Yeah. My birthday is in two weeks."

"I know. You won't be a little kid anymore. That's why I need to tell you about baby hours so you'll be able to use them."

I forgot about being afraid and sat up in the dark to get closer to Luce. My nine-year-old brother who was brave and would keep me safe.

"What are they?"

Luce moved closer to me. "Baby hours are the ones between midnight and when the sun rises. It's the time a new day is getting ready to be born. They're the most special hours of the whole entire day."

"Why?"

He moved even closer. "Because the hours while the new day is getting ready are the best times to think of stuff that makes you happy. Like things you want to happen when it gets all born. And if you think hard enough, you'll see these things in your dreams. Then, if you keep on thinking and thinking about them, you'll be happy that whole new day."

"I could think better if my night-light was on."

Even in the dark it was beginning to seem that I could see Luce sitting there, shaking his head.

"No, Tika, that won't work. For the baby hours to work their magic, it has to be dark. That's the only way the new day can be born. The daylight has to grow from being teeny tiny—too dark to see—to big. Like the sun."

While he sat there, I started doing what my big brother told me to do. I closed my eyes and started thinking about things that made me happy. And I did it the next night. And the night after that. I had done it for so many other nights afterward that I never again was afraid of the dark.

Baby hours . . .

I punch my fist into my pillow.

Now what? Having those kinds of thoughts again will be impossible!

I want to put the pillow over my face and scream into it, but I just punch it again. And again and again.

I'll ignore the baby hours and find something to read.

I rush to get out of bed and almost step on Mr. Jen's tail. I pick the cat up and rub my chin into the soft spot on the top of his head. He looks at me, deciding whether to stay in my arms or not. Then he yawns and I feel his little purr-mobile starting.

Purr-mobile . . .

I jerk my head up so fast it hurts. It's like I'm spastic. Like I believe thoughts I can't stand will spill out through my ears if I move my head hard enough and at the right angle. Then I just stand there, thinking that maybe I should get in bed and try to go to sleep, since I have to go back to school tomorrow. I start thinking that maybe curling up for a while with Mr. Jen will help me relax and am getting ready to do that when I hear Bibi's door click shut. Then I decide that first I should tiptoe across the hall to make sure she's okay.

When I get there, I tap on her door at the same time I'm turning the knob. "Bibi, you okay?"

I stick my head through the opened part of the door. Bibi's in her nightclothes, sitting in the chair by the window. She sees me and smiles. "Come on in."

Mr. Jen jumps out of my arms onto her bed like she invited him to do something.

"Did I wake you, baby?" I shake my head. Bibi smiles. "I'm glad you're here. I want to show you something."

I sit on the floor near Bibi's knees while she digs through the photographs that are everywhere. In her lap, on the table, scattered across the floor, in little piles on her bed.

"I'm going to put together a special family album. One especially for Luce."

Bibi's smiling, even though tears have started running down her cheeks. But seeing them doesn't make me feel uncomfortable. Anyway, I know exactly how she's feeling.

"I thought it would be a good idea to create a family tree memory book. Something to show how each of us in the family is connected to Luce. How he's a big part of all of us, even though we didn't physically . . . well, physically produce him. You know."

Take that, Willa Vernon, you pitiful stupid cow!

I hope my evil feelings don't creep into my voice. "Umhm. That's a great idea, Bibi. Can I help?"

"I was hoping you'd say that. To make this work like I

want it to, the photographs should have writing under them. You know, captions."

"Good idea."

Bibi chuckles. "That's what I think. I also think that my very creative granddaughter who has gotten high marks in English her entire life might be willing to write those captions. Think that's a good idea, too?"

I feel almost like smiling. "Okay, Bibi."

"Between the two of us, we should be able to remember something that connects Luce to everybody in the family." Bibi reaches into the stack on her lap and holds up a picture of Aunt Ingrid, her daughter. Mama's sister. "Like for Ingrid here. Remember the time she was visiting for the weekend and disappeared practically all of Saturday? She and Luce?"

"Yeah. None of us knew they had gone to that sushi place. They ate so much neither of them had room for the big family dinner Dad spent most of the day cooking."

I wonder if Bibi's seeing Aunt Ingrid and Luce like I am. The two of them walking in from lunch at dinnertime, looking more full and happy than guilty.

"More raw than cooked."

"What?" Bibi frowns.

"More raw than cooked. That's what a caption might

say." I look at Bibi, wanting to see a smile replace the frown. It doesn't. "Or maybe not."

Bibi grins. "Keep thinking. You'll come up with something that'll be just right."

She keeps looking through the pictures. Mr. Jen jumps from the bed into my lap. After a minute his purr-mobile is a steady hum.

Bibi holds up another picture. "You won't have any trouble thinking of something to write for this picture. You might even be able to remember a direct quote, although with all his joking around, sometimes my brother says something less than memorable."

I'm reaching for the picture when it hits me what Bibi just said.

Joking around . . . my brother . . .

I realize that Bibi's talking about Brune. Her only living brother. My great-uncle.

My hand falls back down on its own and rests on Mr. Jen's silky fur. I try to keep my mind from going back, but it moves all on its own just like my hand and gathers up a bunch of memories.

Uncle Brune having one too many cocktails at the family reunion and yakking it up with anybody who'll listen. Not paying attention to who's around having to hear his too-loud voice. "You know, I was talking to Luce a while ago. He was telling me about some of the courses he's taking at that college he's in. Sounds like interesting stuff."

A too-loud, coughing laugh. "That Luce is okay. He's turning out to be quite a young man."

Cousin Karen trying to back out the door Uncle Brune has his arm across and looking like she'd rather be anywhere else on earth than there, having to listen to him.

"Yeah, Lexie and Simon lucked out with that store-bought baby."

It all comes back to me. Everything from that day. That awful voice coming through the door where I was waiting on the other side to go through. The way Cousin Karen looked when she saw me outside the door after she finally got away from Uncle Brune. How her soft lawyer-voice sounded when she put her arm around me. "Leah, the First Amendment to our Constitution is a powerful gear in the wheel of our democracy. But sometimes there's irrefutable proof that some people simply should never have learned to speak!"

Remembering, I feel the heat in my chest begin to crawl through my body. Down through my stomach, up through my neck. I clench my fists to keep from snatching the photograph Bibi's holding out of her hand and ripping it into a thousand pieces.

How can any of us be related to anyone so stupid! He belongs in Willa Vernon's family!

"Let's see, maybe I could make a page with Brune, Walker, and some of the other old-timers. I guess I'll have to add me in the group, too. Oh dear. You won't use the word 'old-timers' will you, baby?" Bibi's chuckle is more to herself than me. "I could put a snapshot of Luce in the middle. Maybe you could come up with something about the generations, you know. . . ."

I feel Mr. Jen rubbing his little face against my knee and hope his loud purr-mobile will somehow make Bibi stop.

if everybody starts all that sad talking i'll lose my mind
i will
i absolutely will
everybody saying how sorry they are
over and over and over and over

maybe i ought to wear a sign around my neck
something like
i know you're sorry so please don't tell me
please please please please don't

maybe enough time has passed that everybody has forgotten

i hope my girl knows i'm going to be sticking to her like glue

✳ 7 ✳

DAD GOES ON LAKE SHORE DRIVE TO TAKE ME TO school and keeps his eyes on the road. I keep mine on the lake. Neither of us says anything. When I press the scan button on the radio and stop at a station playing Prince, Dad doesn't even grunt like he normally would.

He hardly says anything, anymore. It's like he's turned into a robot.

Finally we get to my school and the robot speaks.

"You okay?" Dad touches my shoulder when I click open the door on my side of the car and then asks the same thing again. "You okay, Leah?"

I'm afraid of the look I might see in his eyes if I look at him. I answer without looking. "I'm okay, Dad." I push the door open and get out. "Thanks for the ride. See you."

I don't wave when I start down the sidewalk toward school. I don't even look back to make sure my roller pack is balanced on two wheels while I'm pulling it behind me.

I don't do anything that I know will make me want to run after him when I see the car drive off.

Even being with Dad the robot would be better than being here.

Paula's waiting by the outside door, even though the last bell has rung. She comes up to the top step as soon as I reach it.

"Hey, girl." She doesn't even try to hold herself back from hugging me and kissing my cheek. "Come on. You making us late." I don't try to stop myself from holding on to Paula's hand as she pulls me inside with her.

It feels strange walking through the building. Everything is familiar and different at the same time. I feel I should be looking around to see if anything has changed, but I'll look like a weirdy if I do. Anyway, I don't really care if it has.

It helps to keep my eyes on the wide horizontal stripes painted down the middle of the walls opposite the lockers.

Red: administration; blue: freshman corridor; purple: sopho-mores.

We pass by only a few kids. Nobody I know or who knows me well enough to stop and say anything. Most everybody's already in class. Homeroom. I wish it could be like this the whole day.

I walk pretty fast down the corridors, and Paula keeps up with me. We both automatically walk slower when we get to the purple stripe and then stop at two top lockers in the middle of the hall.

"Good old number two thirty-six." Paula twists and opens her combination lock. "Hurry up, Leah. Get going with number two thirty-eight." She starts exchanging books from her backpack with ones in her locker. "And be glad you didn't have to do yesterday's English assignment. Be *very* glad."

I'm surprised when my locker door swings open. I had twisted the knob of the lock without even thinking about the combination and now have the lock in my hand. I stare into the dark, empty cubbyhole, wondering what I should do next.

"Leah?" Paula has an armful of books and is looking at me. Her locker door is shut. "You going to carry that stuff in your roller pack around with you all day?"

I look down at the stuffed roller pack and remember. Paula brought all my books and notebooks from my locker to me last week.

Or was it two weeks ago?

I still can't seem to decide what to do. We have English after homeroom, which we're almost too late to bother with. I don't know where my books for English are because I never even opened the roller pack after Paula brought it to my house.

I'm just standing there, making us later and later when finally one thing occurs to me. "Paula, I got to get things together. I have to get myself organized. You go on."

Paula doesn't move. "You sure? I don't mind waiting, Leah. I really don't."

"I'm sure. Really. I'll catch up with you in English." Feeling tears gathering behind my eyes, I look down at my roller pack.

How am I going to make it through this day?

I keep my eyes on my roller pack. "Please go on, Paula, so you won't be late."

She still stands there for a couple of seconds. Then she plucks the back of my hand softly and goes down the hall.

I lay my roller pack flat on the floor and unzip it. While I'm digging through a pile of loose papers to get to the books, I see feet coming toward me. I stand up right away.

It's Ms. Rice. My guidance counselor from last year.

"Hi, Leah. I hoped I'd run into you today." She puts her hand on my arm. "I'm happy to see you."

"Hi . . . ah . . . um . . ." I try to do something besides sound like an idiot, but the tears behind my eyes are beginning to burn like crazy. I try again. "I'm . . . ah, I'm . . ."

Ms. Rice moves closer and puts her arms around me. The beautiful smell fills my nose.

Patchouli.

Luce had grinned last year when I told him that I had been assigned to Ms. Rice. That she was my freshman counselor. "Good old Patchouli."

"Patchouli? What does that mean?" My brother liked to give special names to people and things. Like naming me "Tika" and our grandmother "Bibi." "Is she awful? Is that what 'patchouli' means?"

"Patchouli, Tika. I'm surprised you haven't heard of it, the way you're into body stuff. It's a scent, an oil, a perfume. Ms. Rice wears it all the time. Nah, she's not awful. Patchouli's actually cool."

And she is. She seems to really care what's going on with you. When she tells you to stop by if you feel you need to talk, you know she means it. Even when you're not a freshman anymore.

And my brother was right about the smell. It's the first thing you notice when you walk into her office. If she passes you in the hall, the soft smell trails behind her like a scarf.

Patchouli.

"Ms. Patchouli." The words slide out of my mouth before I even realize it. Before I can stop myself.

Oh Luce. You could call her that to her face, but not me!

The second I hear what I've said, I want to sink through the floor.

Ms. Rice pulls me closer and rubs her hand back and forth across my shoulders. "Don't ever try to keep the tears from coming, Leah. And know that you're going to miss him forever."

I hear something like a laugh humming in her chest. "But weren't we lucky to have such a wonderful spirit in our lives for the time that we did."

The tears feel hot and burn my eyes like they always do. But now, in some bizarre way, it seems that I'm also smiling.

☙ 8 ❧

I GET TO THE TRACK, WHERE I TOLD PAULA I WOULD meet her. While I'm looking around, I see Coach Beane. He waves and starts toward me.

"Hey, Leah. Good to see you."

"It's good to see you, too." The words come out automatically, the way they have been all day. But they're real when I say them to Coach Beane. He's one of the nicest teachers I have. Besides being the track coach, he teaches honors math for all grades. But most of all, he's cool. He gets kids.

"How'd it go today?" His eyes are soft. I know I don't have to answer.

I shrug my shoulders. He nods his head.

"Hope I'll see you back at the track soon. Whenever you're ready, we'll all be waiting—me and the team." He pats me on my shoulder and heads to the field.

I don't know if I want to get back into track or not. Luce was one of the reasons I went out for track in the first place.

One of the only things I was ever able to beat him at was running. Not swimming. And certainly not chess. He would never play me easy at anything. But I knew how much he wanted me to be good at something. To me the best part of winning on the track was telling Luce about it and knowing how happy he was to hear it.

What difference would it make if I win now—Luce won't be around to be proud.

I kick at the grass and wish I had told Paula I'd meet her at the El station.

I need to leave here.

I think I see Paula on the other side of the field. I start to wave when I notice one of the kids on the field doing practice runs.

Lester!

My arm freezes in the air like something grabbed it. My stomach starts churning and everything about Lester runs across my mind. Everything.

At first Lester was mostly the sophomore in the awesome leather jacket who always sat near the back at Monday assembly. He started being more that day Paula and I watched him doing laps and I mentioned how cute I thought he was.

"Lester Evans? Cute?"

"Come on, Paula. He's cute. Admit it. And that leather jacket is the bomb."

"Everything Lester puts on his back is tight. Dressing is his thing. But I don't need to admit anything about how Lester Evans looks. He has that conversation too much with himself already."

"He should, as cute as he is." I was teasing Paula more than anything else, but it was true.

"Leah, you can do a whole lot better than Lester Evans. A *whole* lot!"

"Okay. Just tell me what's so wrong with Lester Evans. Besides being, you know, *adorable*-looking, he's one of the stars of the track team, a *GQ* dresser, and has his own wheels."

"And a good kisser. Don't forget that."

I almost fell over. "Paula, have you been holding out on me?"

"Girl, please! Me and Lester Evans? Not even in my nightmares." Paula made a face. "That's the word from Alyssia Barksdale."

"Alyssia Barksdale? That's who Lester goes with?"

"They did over the summer. I don't know about now. They're really a matched set, though. Probably spend their alone time gazing into twin mirrors and comparing notes."

I had laughed with Paula that day, even though I didn't

agree with what she was saying. Not about Lester, anyhow. Anyway, I wanted to find out for myself.

Being out for track made it easy to get Lester's attention. Every day I managed to be in his general area for warm-ups, and after about a week he made sure he was in mine.

After the day Lester took me home in his father's little foreign job—his car was in the shop—I got even more interested. That was the day Mama asked six million questions and tried to pass three million rules, starting with who were his parents, why would any responsible adult let a barely sixteen-year-old drive around such an expensive car, and how she would prefer me to continue to take the train home and let the young man visit me there.

Luce was home and answered the phone one night when Lester called. "Come on, Tika," he teased. "Tell the truth. Do you really *like* being called 'LeeLee'?"

"How's that different from being called 'Tika'? That's not my name either."

Luce laughed. "Oh, it's different, Tika-LeeLee. Trust me. Real different."

I didn't care what anybody said. Not even Paula, who usually rolled her eyes and shook her head whenever I happened to mention anything that had to do with Lester. Like I wouldn't be going on the train because he was driving me home.

But after a while—actually, only a little while—I wondered why I *did* keep hanging with Lester. He was cute, but not much fun away from the track. Or really interesting anywhere. To him it was more than enough to have his own car and all the other stuff he talked his parents into getting for him. Stuff that he liked to brag about.

Maybe I just wanted to see if the kissing part was true.

Now, standing there at the track, watching him get closer to me, the memory of being with Lester when . . . that day . . . floods my mind. The two of us at Lincoln Park Zoo. Both of us standing near the waterfall where the polar bears are. Me telling Lester I didn't want to get my hair wet.

Lester grinning. "Don't worry, LeeLee. No way am I gonna let a fine dime like you get wet. No way."

Now I want to run. Fast. To get so far away I won't be able even to hear Lester calling me. Even if he hollers at the top of his lungs. But I know I can't. Now he's almost in my face.

"Hi, Lester."

"LeeLee. I been trying to catch up with you all day."

He gets closer. I move back a step. "Ah . . . yeah . . . well . . ."

"You probably have a lot to catch up on. Yeah. A lot." He moves two steps closer.

I move two steps back. "Yeah, a lot."

"I, ah, tried to call you . . . I mean, I *started* to call you a couple of times but I figured it might be a bad time to . . ."

It might *be a bad time?*

When Lester moves still one more step closer, I stay where I am. I look into his clueless face and wonder what on earth I had been thinking of. Why in the world I had ever wanted to be with him.

To tell the truth, I really hate *being called "LeeLee." I despise it.*

I look straight into his face. "Lester, thanks for coming over to say hi, but I have to go. Like you said, it's a bad time and I have a lot to catch up on. It's going to take me weeks. Probably months. Maybe even the rest of high school!"

I grip the handle of my roller pack tight so it will move with me. So I won't stumble over it while I back away from Lester.

"See you around."

Then I turn around and head to the other end of the field where I hope it really is Paula that I saw on the other side and that she's all set to go because if she's not I'm leaving anyhow. I move as fast as I can without actually running. I have to get away before Lester can say anything else to me. Before I have to say to his face that I never want to hear that name "LeeLee" again. Ever.

❧ 9 ❧

"HEY, GIRL."

Paula is out of breath when she finally catches up with me at the corner of the second block after school. But she falls into step with me without asking why I didn't wait for her at the track. Why I tore out like somebody crazy without bothering to come all the way to the other end of the field where she was waiting.

She smiles, but not wide enough to make her dimples deeper. "You survived."

"Yep. I survived." I want to smile back, but it feels strange even trying.

We continue down the other two blocks without saying much of anything. Just a little about the display in the window of the sports store when we pass it. There's always something new and cool to notice there.

At the El station, it's quiet on the platform. There's only a few other kids waiting for the train like us, talking and laughing loud every now and then. Noise like a radio being turned up and then down again. I know Paula doesn't mind us standing there quiet.

Then I hear the train not too far away and know I need to tell Paula before it gets closer. "I'm never going out with Lester again."

"Huh?"

Not expecting me to say anything, she wasn't paying attention. The train's getting closer.

I say it louder. "I'm never seeing Lester again. You know, going out with him."

Paula grins. I wonder if it's because I'm talking so loud. I hope nobody else heard me. "That's good news." Paula's dimples get deeper. "That Lester—on the track he's fantastic. But off the field, well, the boy definitely has turkey tendencies."

"Yep, a real gobble-gobble."

Paula laughs. It's clear above the noise of the train pulling into the station. "Anyway, he's not right for you. Not even close to right." She's almost yelling so I can hear her over the conductor's voice calling out stations. "You know, like Aaron James would be. Now there's somebody I think—"

I'm shaking my head while I push Paula ahead of me to get on the train and find seats. At the same time I can't keep from paying attention to the quick little pictures of Aaron James that flash through my head.

Aaron. Looking like a clumsy duck that first day I saw *him* on the track.

"That's the new kid," Nicholas Simms said from behind me where he was standing. "I heard he's here on a scholarship. Sure hope it's not for track."

Aaron James. A serious face lugging a big pack of books. Smiling on the poster of candidates running for student council and looking almost like a different person. That same smiling face looking at me over his date's head at the sophomore dance and me sneaking a look back over Lester's shoulder.

When I feel myself almost smiling now, I wish it felt okay.

❧ IO ❧

"What are you watching?"

I jump when I hear Mama's voice behind me, not realizing she's come into the den. Dad looks up from his crossword puzzle. "I've not been paying attention. Leah, what's on?"

I know Dad's just been holding the newspaper and staring at the crossword puzzle and that Mama probably knows it and is asking me about what's on TV because I'm the only one in the room even *trying* to stay conscious. I feel like yelling at both of them.

Dad, what's the point of being a robot? Like you can only act if somebody else pushes your buttons? Mama, why are you asking me what's on? Why don't you ask your husband?

But I don't say anything. I just shrug my shoulders. "Nothing special."

"What channel?" Mama sits on the couch. Near the end next to Dad's chair. The television is right in her face and the station logo is in the corner of the screen. I don't feel like I need to answer.

Mama looks at me. "Leah, what channel are you watching?"

I want to tell her it's the same one she's looking at but before I can say anything, she keeps going. "Leah, there's no reason to act like this."

I try to keep from saying anything. Especially what's right at the front of my brain. But something slips out anyway. "Like what?"

Then Dad jumps in before Mama answers. "Lexie, let's not . . . please."

Mama doesn't stop looking at me. Staring with her forever-sad eyes. Forever sad *dry* eyes. I don't look away from her either, while she tries to keep from folding her arms across her chest, something she usually does when she's trying to hide that she's getting mad. Like making sure her voice sounds all calm, which she's also doing now.

"We're still a family, Leah, and we need to act like it."

What family, Mama? You and me and Dad? And Bibi? Because that's all the family there is. And I don't think that's enough for anybody. Especially you! But it's not my fault and not a reason you should be getting on my *case.*

The words are pounding in my head so bad, my head begins to hurt. But I don't move or say anything.

Dad jumps in again. This time he puts his not-even-looked-at paper down. "Lexie, come on now. It's hard for everybody. For all of us."

"Hard?" Mama's head jerks around like somebody snatched a string attached to her nose. "Hard, Simon? It's impossible!"

Mama's voice cracks. Like she's about to break down. She stands up and Dad does the same thing right behind her. "Simon, I just don't know how . . ."

I can't make out the rest of what she's saying because Dad puts his arm around her and pulls her head to his chest. I wonder if she's about to cry but can't tell because I can't see her face. Dad reaches out for me with his other arm but I shake my head. I keep shaking it while I get up and leave the room.

At least they're *family. They have each other.*

I stand in front of the door of Luce's room. For a minute Mr. Jen, who followed me from the den, stands there with me. Then he turns around and walks away.

Not a place you want to be, huh, Jen-Jen. . . .

The door is so empty now. The "Wanted" poster and karate magazine cover with Luce's face on them have been removed. They were fakes but looked real. Luce got them at

Universal Studios when Grandma Myrtle took us there a couple of summers ago.

As usual, the door is closed. Sometimes I open it and leave it that way on purpose. I want to see if Mama's deliberately keeping it shut. She is.

Just like she used to sometimes when Luce wouldn't clean up his room for weeks.

I open the door, go inside, and close the door behind me.

Although things have been straightened up, most of the stuff is like Luce left it. Except for his freshwater aquarium. Dad donated that to a high school.

The Dungeons & Dragons books are stacked on the bookshelves with a few of the weird playing pieces scattered nearby.

"Come on, Tika. Just try it with me. D and D is the king of 'let's pretend' games. You'd love it!"

There are more fantasy books on the shelves, stuffed in among the odd assortment of biology textbooks Luce would buy from secondhand stores. Hanging near one of them is a two-sided drawing of a hip bone.

"How come you've drawn the same thing twice?"

"On one side is the drawing I copied from a biology book. The other drawing is from my head."

"They look the same to me."

"That's because you're not a scientist like me."

"You're not a scientist either."

"I will be, Tika-Tika. Someday I will be."

His trophies are all together, covering the entire top of his bureau. The tall ones he won for karate are lined across the back. Like soldiers. The trophies he won for chess are stacked in front.

Luce kept his trophies in different places all over the room. His favorite—the one shaped like a black king chess piece—was always on the little table beside his bed.

"This is proof, Tika. A-one, in my class. A-ONE!"

The only thing on the little table now is the picture of Luce, Mama, and me. The one taken on Mother's Day the year the three of us went to the Shedd to celebrate.

Mama's rule about Mother's Day was for each of us to write on a piece of paper an activity we wanted to do, toss all the papers into a bag, and then let her pick one. "It's children who make Mother's Day possible, so this is the only fair way we can decide what to do together."

That year she picked Luce's choice, the one he always wanted and wrote down: "Let's go to the aquarium!"

Dad dropped the three of us off at the Shedd and was waiting outside with his camera when we came out. In the picture he took, I have on the new dolphin T-shirt Mama bought for me, and Luce is wearing that silly dolphin cap she bought for him. His grin is so wide it looks like his eyes have almost disappeared. He's pointing at Mama, who's holding up her arms with her hands face up.

"In case you're wondering, Dad, Mama's the only one who didn't get a gift!"

On Luce's bulletin board, all his notes to himself and schedules he would put up but never bother to look at have been taken down. The only things left are the Halloween pictures.

Luce as a pumpkin clown when he was about two or three. It's the only picture of him in a costume that somebody bought. All the other costumes are ones Luce put together himself. The knight costume where he's wearing the cape he asked Bibi to stitch together for him. She used an old velvet evening cape she wore when she was young. That same year he conned Mama out of her old silver evening gown and made it into a tunic by cutting a big round opening at the top and V-shapes all around the bottom.

"You were only three that year, Tika. I tried to talk Mama and Dad into letting you be my little pet dragon, but they wouldn't. Too bad, don't you think? I bet you would have liked being a pet dragon."

In one of the pictures he's dressed as a mummy. That was the year he couldn't finish making the trick-or-treat rounds and ended up with barely half a bag of candy.

"Shoot! These darn strips of that old sheet keep unraveling. Shoot! I should have used tape like Dad said."

I unpin the photograph that's my favorite. Luce dressed as Gandhi. I take it down.

"Gandhi was a fantastic human being, Tika. The original peacenik."

I'm holding the picture so tightly in my fingers it begins to crack a little. When I loosen my fingers, it slips out and lands on the floor. I want to take it to my room and put it on my bulletin board, but seeing it lying there next to my shoe makes me decide the falling was a sign to leave the picture here. I pick it up and pin it back with the others.

You were a fantastic human being, too, Luce. The most fantastic person in my life.

I close my eyes to get the smell. The smell I imagine every time I come into my brother's room. It was so strong at first, it was like he had just stepped into the closet. With my eyes shut, it's easy for me to believe that the scent is still there.

Luce. Oh Luce . . .

❁ ❁ ❁

This time I shut the door behind me when I leave Luce's room. On my way down the hall I pass Bibi's room, where the door is open. She's watching television with Mr. Jen asleep in her lap. I tip by without bothering either of them. When I get to my room, I close the door as quietly as I can.

Even though my door is shut tight, I try not to make a single sound when I reach under my mattress for Luce's papers. The ones I took out of his room the day . . . the day it happened. They're all kinds of papers—old assignments, exams, sketches, reports. Some are letters he never finished or didn't send. I haven't read the letters. Not yet. Maybe I never should. I don't know.

I have the papers in two piles under my mattress. I pull out a sheet from the main pile—the big one—and see that it has writing on both sides. I read some of it.

"The purpose of this lab is to determine the amounts of sand and sugar in an unknown mixture. This is to be accomplished with a separating technique using water. The water should mix with the sugar, leaving only sand behind. . . ."

I know from the date on the paper that Luce wrote this during his first year in college. I fold the sheet in half and push it into the second pile under the mattress. That's the pile with my notes or those sheets of Luce's I decided not to use. It's the pile I'll burn to cinders before I'll let anybody get their hands on it to read anything.

I pull out another sheet from the main pile. On this one, one side is blank. I take it to my desk.

I haven't figured out why it's easier to write to myself on these sheets of paper instead of in my little notebook. The one Bibi made a needlepoint cover for and that I keep in the locked drawer of my desk. All I know is that it *is* easier.

The first time I wrote on the back of a sheet that had Luce's drawing of a knee, I thought maybe I was going a little crazy. I still wonder if I am, but I really don't care. All I know is that every time I write on one of his papers, I feel just a tiny bit better. A tiny bit like one day I just might get over wishing I had been in that stupid awful car right along with my brother.

you're right Mama
it *is* impossible
for everybody
for you and Dad and Bibi and Grandma Myrtle and
Mahri and Cliff and
me me me me me ME!

we all loved him so so so so so so so much
it's impossible to even think of losing that much
poured out love

but we did

there's somebody else who lost him too
somebody who doesn't even know it
just like they don't know how wonderful he turned out
to be

they don't know because they gave him away

gave him away
gave him away
AWAY

who would do that?
who?
?????????????????

✖ II ✖

EVEN BEFORE I WALK INTO HER ROOM AND SEE WHAT'S on the screen, I can tell Bibi's watching one of those black-and-white movies. It's how the characters sound in their singsongy, high voices. "Oh, Charlotte, my darling. Whatever shall I do? It pains me to see you so unhappy. I simply cannot *bear* it!" The music's a giveaway, too. Soupy. Like something being poured out instead of played.

I stop at my grandmother's door. "Hey, Beebs, I have a deal for you. If you're watching something in black-and-white, you'll hand over ten dollars to me. If it's in color, I do the same for you. Bet?"

"Shhhhh!" Bibi shushes me like she's annoyed. But she's not. I see that little smile when I flop down on her bed.

Sometimes it seems that Bibi's room is the only sane place left in our apartment. I can almost feel normal when I'm there, with her. As normal as I'm probably ever going to feel again.

"So who is it today, Bibi? Loretta Young? Bette Davis? My auntie's namesake, Ingrid Bergman, or somebody else?" Everybody in the family teases Bibi about her favorite "stars of the silver screen," as she calls the old actresses. All of them are dead, but in Bibi's room they're alive and well. They're about the only thing she watches on the little TV Aunt Ingrid brought for her room. Bibi doesn't even know who most of the current movie stars are.

"No, Luce. I never heard of her."

"Aw, come on, Bibi, baby, you got *to know who Sanaa Lathan is. She's hot!"*

"Hot? What's that mean?"

"Bibi, please join us in this century. Try it. You'll like it. . . ."

Hearing Luce's teasing voice makes me miss most of what Bibi is saying. "Huh? I mean, what did you say, Bibi?"

"I sa*aaaaaaa*id . . ." Bibi draws out the word like I do sometimes. "I think you might enjoy this movie. It has quite an interesting story line."

"What's it about?"

"Does that mean you'd like to watch it?" Bibi wiggles her eyebrows, giving me one of those fake surprised looks.

I move myself to the opposite end of the bed so I can see the screen. "Better hurry up and tell me. You're missing your movie."

"Oh, I've seen this many times." Bibi settles back in her chair, happy like always to have somebody to share one of "her" movies. "It's called *The Old Maid*—"

"Wow. Great title."

Bibi ignores me. "Bette Davis stars as Charlotte, a woman who agrees to gives up her illegitimate child for adoption and then must watch the new family . . ."

Adoption?

I look over at Bibi, expecting her to be looking back at me. But her eyes stay on the screen while she keeps explaining. "The adoptive mother is Delia, Charlotte's cousin. It happens that at one time Charlotte and Delia had been in love with the same man—the man who turns out to be the father of the child, Tina. One of the interesting twists is that Tina doesn't know—"

"Shhhhh." I roll closer to the end of the bed so the screen is directly in front of me. Bibi's got me hooked.

I stay in Bibi's room for hours. After *The Old Maid* ends, the host makes an announcement about the next movie, *To Each His Own.* "Unwed and left alone, the young mother gives up her child for adoption. . . ."

"Bibi, what's going on? Is this channel having some kind of adoption fest?"

She laughs. "Actually, you might call it that. This network often explores certain themes—you know, shows movies about the same thing all evening." She looks at me over the top of her glasses. "Don't tell me *you're* interested in seeing *more* of these oldies."

I ignore my grandmother's sarcasm like she ignored mine. I turn back to the screen and get settled again. The next movie's about to start.

It's almost midnight when the second movie ends. Bibi's in bed, reading. She decided after about a half hour that seeing it about a month ago had been enough for her. For the time being, anyway. "But it's a good movie, Leah. Olivia De Havilland won her first Oscar for her role."

I hadn't asked anymore about who that actress was because I didn't want to miss anything. Bibi was right about the movie being good. It was a great story, even with the sappy ending.

But now I wanted to talk. To ask Bibi about these movies. If she thinks the stories are at all realistic.

Do you think Luce's birth mom was like that Josephine Norris in the movie? That she gave up her baby only because she didn't want people to know he was illegitimate? Do you think that's how people feel today?

"Bibi?"

"Hmmm?" Bibi lowers her book, yawning. "I think I'm falling asleep with this book in my hands." She yawns again. "Did you want something?" She smiles at me. It's easy to see that she's bushed.

"Only to say thanks, Beebs." I get up from her chair, where I had curled up after she got up to do other things. "It was fun watching some of your silver screen wonders." I bend over to kiss her on the head. "'Night, Bibi."

"'Night, sweetheart. See you in the morning."

Once I get to my room and start getting ready for bed, the questions take over. They fill up my mind while I finish unbraiding my hair and changing into my pj's. I feel like I can almost see them in the bathroom mirror while I'm brushing my teeth and washing my face. When I pick up Mr. Jen to make sure he's safe in my room before I shut my door, he looks back at me like *he's* heard them.

Do most adoptions happen like they show in the movies—people giving away their kid because they have to or feel they should for the sake of the child? Does everybody who gives a child away spend the rest of their lives wishing they hadn't? Did Luce's parents?

I sit on the edge of my bed and notice it's almost one o'clock. I have an early schedule tomorrow and know I'd better get to sleep fast, but I can't turn off the questions.

Did Luce want to find his birth parents? Did he ever try?

Then, just as I reach over to turn out my light, I remember.

The essay! The one Luce wrote for his college application.

I jump out of bed, start digging under my mattress for the main pile of papers, and all of it comes back.

It was the night before the absolute last day the application could be mailed to meet the deadline. Mama and Luce had been battling about the application all day and were still at it in the kitchen after dinner.

"Look, Ma, I don't see anything wrong with my essay. The directions told me to write about a fact of my life that had a great effect on me, and that's what I wrote."

"Luce, I *know* what you wrote. And the reason I know is because you left your file open on the computer after you finished, knowing full well I was waiting for you to finish to use it."

"Okay. So it was my way of letting you read the essay without asking you to. Anyway, how was I to know you really wanted to read it. You never asked."

"Luce." Mama had that kind of tired-soft voice. "Luce, don't even *try* to go there. You *knew* I wanted to read your essay. And you wanted me to. That's why you left the file open. So I could."

Mama walked up behind Luce. "Look, son, I'm not saying your essay is bad—it's a little stiff, standoffish, but not bad." She pressed her head against his back. "But it's not the best you can do. That you *should* do. You're going for early decision, remember. Early decision at a tough school to get into."

Luce didn't move. He spoke to Mama like she was standing there in front of him and not leaning against his back.

"So I'll take another look at it. Will you be satisfied then?"

From where I was standing near the back door, it sounded like Mama chuckled. "Partly." Mama put her hands on Luce's shoulders. "What would satisfy me more would be for you to reconsider your topic. I think—"

Luce whirled around so fast, it cut Mama off and made her wobble when she stepped back. He reached to catch her arm. "Listen, Ma, if you think I'm going to start over, you must be—"

Mama held up Luce's hand that was holding hers and put it over his mouth. "Luce, all I said was 'reconsider.' It's your choice, son. Completely."

Luce rolled his eyes away from Mama's face. Then he turned away his whole face.

Mama didn't let that stop her. "I just have one more thing

to say. Being an adopted child is *definitely* a life-influencing fact, and one that would *definitely* set you *and* your essay apart from some of the applicants."

Luce didn't say anything else. He just walked out of the kitchen, shaking his head the whole time. But Mama had made her point. I figured it when I saw him headed to Dad's office and heard him typing on the computer. I knew it for certain when Luce told Mama at breakfast that she'd better feed her nosey habit before he sealed up his application.

He wrote about being adopted in that essay.

I drag out the big pile of papers from under my mattress and spread them across my bed. Luce's papers.

Maybe he printed out a copy of his essay to save and stuffed it in one of the folders I emptied.

I look through the whole pile. At every single sheet. The baby hours are almost over when I finally decide that what I want to find isn't there. But all while I'm looking, I'm thinking that maybe not being able to get it off my mind is some kind of sign.

✣ 12 ✣

I MAKE IT ONTO THE TRAIN AT THE LAST MINUTE AND barely get my roller pack inside before the doors slide shut. I land right beside Hat Lady. That's the name Paula and I have given the woman who wears a srange assortment of hats. A *truly* strange assortment. They're usually different but *always* more than a little strange. Today's version is a purple knit pull-on with a pink ball swinging from a red string attached to the pointy top.

I'm starting to turn away so I won't end up laughing in her face when I notice that today Hat Lady is holding a kid's hand. Her son. He has to be because he looks just like her. My almost-laugh becomes a smile for the little kid.

A picture of the little kid's face stays in my mind when I turn around to walk down the aisle to look for Paula. How, even without anything weird on his head, he looks so much like his mom I didn't have to wonder for a second who he might be.

No question about him *not being adopted.*

I yank my roller pack, telling myself to get all this adoption stuff off my mind and start walking on my toes, trying to spot Paula in the crowd of people.

I wonder if Luce looked that much like his birth mom?

I'm almost praying that everything I have to do in school today will force me to think about anything else but that.

Paula's looking for me in the other direction. I manage to get behind her and say, "Boo!" before she sees me. She jumps and laughs at the same time. "You crazy, girl." We laugh together.

Being with Paula is my other safe place to be. Like with Bibi, I can be myself with Paula, whatever that happens to be. I can settle in with her. I don't even *try* to imagine what I would do without her.

"How come you so late? That's *my* trick." Paula has to talk above the noise of the train. "What's going on?"

"Had a late night. Got off to a slow start this morning."

"Anything wrong?"

I'm about to shake my head when it occurs to me that talking with Paula about what I can't seem to shake off my mind might be a good thing. But not here with strangers around and all the wheel and tunnel noises. So I hold up my finger and mouth, "In a minute." She gets it right away.

In a way I wish the noise of the wheels click-clacking their way down the heavy tracks would take over my brain. But it doesn't. The questions keep rushing through.

Why am I even *thinking* about Luce being adopted? That kind of thinking makes me as bad as that awful Vernon woman and silly Uncle Brune! No. Never. Shut up, shut *up*!

I look through the smudged, dingy windows of the train. The sun is full, bright, even through them.

I bet Luce wondered about it more than he acted like he did. He might have even thought about finding his birth parents. Did he ever try on his own? Without telling any of us?

We're getting close to our stop. I clinch the handle of my roller pack tighter, ready to move with the crowd.

It's not like I have any questions about him being my brother. My *real* brother. Luce will always be that. Just like I will always be his *real* sister. Bibi will be his *real* grandmother. And Mama and Dad his *real* parents.

The wheels make a long screech as the train pulls into the station.

But the fact is, there were other parents. And maybe *somebody* should try to find out who they were.

✿ ✿ ✿

Our stop is three blocks from school. Even though both of us have early schedules today, it's so nice outside we automatically walk slower than we should. At first neither of us says much of anything. I know Paula's waiting for me to tell her what I said I would. Then before we get to the end of the first block, I decide to get it over with.

"Paula, there's something I'm thinking I should do. But after I tell you, you have to promise to tell me whether or not you think I'm nuts. Promise?"

My words spill out. I know I don't have to wait for Paula to say she promises before I keep on and I don't. "I'm thinking about trying to find out who Luce's biological parents are. Were, I mean. Actually, they're probably still alive so maybe I should say 'are' even though Luce is . . . is . . ." The spilling stops.

After hearing myself say the words out loud, I let out a big breath. It's one I've probably been holding in ever since last night, right after that second movie ended.

Or maybe even the night before that when I wrote myself that note.

Now, even though I'm standing there, waiting to see what Paula will say, I feel relieved.

"Like Antwone Fisher! Leah, is that what gave you the idea?" Paula's big eyes get bigger.

"Who?"

"Antwone Fisher. You know, the guy in Denzel's movie. The one about the navy guy who goes searching for his parents."

"Oh . . . yeah." It comes back to me.

Usually I go to any and every movie that has Denzel Washington's name anywhere on it, but I had too much homework that night when Mama, Dad, and Bibi decided to see *Antwone Fisher*. Mama and Bibi are like me. They want to see anything Denzel is in. Dad wanted to see the movie because it's the first picture Denzel Washington directed.

Afterward Dad teased Mama about how much she had cried during the movie. "You should have seen your mother, although 'heard' would be a more accurate verb. She actually sobbed out loud. The woman sitting in front of us turned around when the lights came up and asked Lexie if she had been the one making all that noise."

"You need to quit, Simon!" Mama was embarrassed. "All the woman said was that she could tell the person behind her was feeling the same way as she. Sad. Anyway, admit it, Simon. You were crying, too."

"Maybe a tear or two. But I definitely wasn't sobbing like someone else we know was."

Now, thinking about what Dad had said, I wonder if Mama had been thinking about Luce when she saw the movie. Luce wasn't . . . he was alive then, but maybe she was thinking about him and his biological parents.

Was she afraid that his feelings about us might change if he found them?

"You saw the movie, right?" Paula stops at the corner where we have to wait for the light.

"No. I missed it. I'll catch it on cable." I bump my roller pack over the curb.

"I thought you said you saw it."

"Nope. Maybe you remember me saying something about my parents going to see it."

"Girl, you should rent it. It's been out on video." Paula kicks at a rock on the sidewalk. "Did . . . ah, do you know if Luce saw it?"

I shrug my shoulders and hum, "I don't know."

We pass the yard where the puny-looking dog sits behind a locked gate. Even his little growl is pitiful.

"Leah, did, ah . . . did Luce want to find his birth parents?"

I decide not to say anything about how much all of it has been on my mind. For hours last night before I finally fell asleep. This morning while I made up my bed and smoothed the covers a quintillion times to make sure, like I always do, that there're no mattress lumps, anywhere. While I stared into my bowl of granola and out the dirty train windows.

I just shrug my shoulders again. "We never talked about it much."

We pass the sports store and, even though we don't have much time, stop to look in. It's like part of our routine.

Our reflections are right in the middle of the purple display window. I want to smile at the short girl in sunglasses under a head full of bouncy curls just above her stuffed backpack. I think about making a face at the other girl, the tall one wearing regular glasses and pulled-back half braids and holding the handle of a stuffed roller pack. One really cute girl so stacked that practically any guy breathing turns around to watch after she passes by. One almost skinny girl with not much to watch in any area.

Through the reflections I ask Paula again. "So, am I nuts?"

Paula answers the same way. "Uh-uh. I don't think so. Not at all. I'll even help, if you want."

Just like that? It's not such a crazy thing to think about doing?

I feel myself relaxing a little. Then I smile and nod my head at the Paula in the window-mirror before we keep going down the last block.

Even though I had the longest day of my week, I'm determined to get the movie. It's a perfect night to watch it. Mama and Dad are at a condo association meeting, and Bibi is out with her book club group.

By the time I get to the video store, it's really crowded. I almost leave automatically. That's what I always do when there're a lot of people in line and ganging up around the shelves, deciding what they want to watch.

But I don't. I squeeze through the crowd to get to the shelves where they keep the dramas. Then I see it.

Antwone Fisher.

There are two or three DVD copies but no videotapes. The one videotape copy seems to have been checked out.

I keep telling Dad we need a DVD player.

Then I see the videotape copy. It's so perfectly lined up behind the slipcase box, it's almost hidden.

A sign.

I grab it, check inside to make sure it's the right movie, and head for one of the checkout lines. I do it just in time.

"Heck. I don't see any more *Antwone Fisher* tapes. Only DVDs."

The lady talking had come into the store behind me. I noticed her because of the hair. It's the same color and length as Mahri's. Not as pretty, though.

I wonder who she's talking to and hope it's not me. Then I hear another voice.

"That movie's gonna be on cable soon. We can see it then."

"I'm tired of waiting for movies to come on cable. And you can see for yourself that most of the new movies here are on DVD and not tape. I keep telling you we need to just go on and get a DVD player. We might as well quit coming here if we don't."

I hold my tape tighter and move closer to the person in front of me in line.

Yep, definitely *a sign.*

❧ 13 ❦

IT'S ALMOST TIME FOR ME TO MEET PAULA FOR LUNCH when I finally get one of the computer stations in the library. I had waited near the one where Wendy Roberts was working, positive that she was about to finish whatever she was doing. Especially since she kept looking up and smiling at me every half minute. Almost like she was apologizing for taking so long and was rushing to get off.

Finally the guy across from Wendy logs off and I get that station. While I'm logging on, I notice Wendy still looking over and giving me that same look.

That's a "poor Leah" look she's been giving me all along.

I stare into the screen, determined not to even glance in Wendy's direction anymore. But now that I'm sitting here and have the screen in front of me, I don't know where I should begin.

Go for basic.

I type "adoption" in the search box. In less than a second

the top of the screen shows that there are over thirty million results!

This could take forever.

I look down the first page.

National Adoption Center

About Adoption

Adoption.org

Adoption Services

I know after reading only a few entries that my beginning wasn't so smart. I back up to the search page and start again, typing "finding birth parents." This time the response lists over two million results. I start reading down the first entries.

Begin with a Free Search

Find Your Birth Family

How to Find Your Birth Parents

Resources for Seeking Birth Parents

All right!

I click on the first entry. A form asking for information comes up. And the first thing you have to do is type in a name.

Of course. What was I thinking? I guess not *thinking is more like it. Just like not* knowing *what Luce's birth parents' name was. Is.*

I click on some of the other entries and see that I have to supply a name for just about all of them to get anywhere.

Look, I don't know *the birth name! If I did, I could start by looking in a telephone book.*

I glance at the clock. It's ten minutes after twelve. Past the time I told Paula I'd be at the cafeteria. I hurry to try one last thing.

Under one of the listings is something about adoptees born in a certain year. I go back to the search page and type "adoptees born in 1984." This time the first response makes me think I might finally be getting somewhere.

Male Adoptees Born Between 1982 and 1984

Yes!

I'm so excited I click on it about five times, bringing the linking page up but taking it back out. I back up and try again, and this time I get it.

Massachusetts Registry of Male Adoptees Born

Between 1982 and 1984

But it would be the Illinois Registry I'll need to check. Mama and Dad wouldn't have gone all the way to Massachusetts to adopt a baby.

I know I'll have to come back later to get the specifics I need, but want to read just a little to get an idea of what to expect when I *do* find the Illinois registry.

I start scrolling down, trying to read as fast as I can. But the more I see, the slower I *have* to go.

This is amazing.

I know I have to hurry or I'll miss lunch altogether, but I can't pull my eyes away from the screen. It's like they're attached to it. And what's really weird, the more I read, the more fascinated and depressed I get, exactly at the same time!

One thing's for sure. Unless I have a specific name, I'm not going to get anything useful online!

❧ 14 ❧

"Some of the messages people had posted were kind of pitiful, you know?"

"Like how?"

"Like one from an adopted kid that said 'I was born with a birthmark on my shoulder. I just want to know who you are.' And one from a birth parent with 'Rita is searching. I just want you to know that I love you.'"

Paula shakes her head. "Yeah, that is kind of pitiful." She unscrews the cap from her bottled water, takes a swig, then screws the top back on. "And you said there were hundreds of listings like that? From both sides?"

"Yep."

Both of us sit there for a minute, not saying anything. Even so, I'd be willing to bet real money that both of us are thinking the same thing.

Is there a message somewhere out there on the Web that someone hopes Luce will read?

Paula unscrews the cap from her bottled water again, takes another swig, then screws the top back on. Again.

I take the last sip from my carton of milk. My grilled cheese with only two missing bites looks greasier than ever, now that it's cold. "Anyway, even to put up one of those pitiful messages you have to have some kind of name."

"So, get a name. Ask your parents for it. They must have some kind of birth information about Luce."

I push my tray away. "I can't."

"Can't what? Ask your parents? Why not?" Paula starts unscrewing the cap from her bottled water. "You have to. It's the only way you're going to find out anything." She takes a long swig, then screws the top back on. *Again.*

"I don't want to say anything to *anybody* about this. Not yet, anyhow. But especially not to my parents."

No way are they ready for this. No way! I don't even know if I am.

I look down at the notes I made while I was online, thinking maybe there was something I hadn't paid enough attention to.

"Too bad you can't go to the attic in your house and look through a musty old trunk that's kept under the eaves." Paula puts her hand on the bottle cap. "You know, like in *Little Women.*"

"Nobody did that in *Little Women*. They searched their trunk for playacting stuff. And Jo used it to write on."

"I know that. I just mean the trunk thing in general. You know, having something packed with mysterious stuff locked away in the attic."

"Great idea, Paula, except for one tiny fact. Our house is a big apartment on one floor and doesn't have an attic."

"I know, I know. But finding something like secret papers in an old trunk would be kind of cool." She's starting to unscrew the bottle cap when I snatch the bottle from her.

"Paula, you're making me crazy!" I finish unscrewing the cap and pour the water in my unused plastic cup. "Here. Now you can just drink without all that extra effort."

Paula stares at me while her hands are still in the air. Like the water bottle is still in them. "I can't believe you did that. What's wrong with me drinking from the bottle?"

"What's wrong with you drinking from the cup?"

Paula keeps looking at me and then bursts out laughing. I can't keep from laughing either. "I guess that was a little extreme. Sorry, girl."

"No harm done." Paula takes a sip from the cup. "Yeech! Now it's only water. Not *bottled* water. It just ain't the same."

"Come on. I'll get you another bottle." I get up from the lunchroom table. "You can slide it into your backpack and open and close it to your heart's content through all your afternoon classes."

"That's okay. I'll empty my little cup and take it along for the memory of water." Paula dumps the water in the fountain we pass on the way out of the lunchroom. "By the way, you ought to begin that *other* investigation, too, you know."

"What are you talking about?"

"Not a 'what.' A 'who.' Aaron James."

"What about Aaron James?"

"Stay with me, Leah. Put it together. I'm saying you should add Aaron James to the list of things to find out about."

We reach the beginning of the purple stripe. "Paula—"

"Listen, girl. I know that finding out about Luce is really important to you now. And I know it's no joke. And that's not what I'm doing now either, you know, joking."

Paula steps in front of me before we reach our lockers. I have to stop walking. "Leah, Aaron's been asking me about you for weeks. Before you came back . . . you know, after everything. Since you've been back, his inquiries have shifted into high gear."

I don't know how to react. I just stand there.

"He's really interested in you, Leah, and he's a nice guy. Really tight."

"Paula—" I try again and have to stop.

"Just think about it. While we're in chemistry, I'll think about water and you think about Aaron. Me water, you Aaron. Water, Aaron. Two essential elements. Okay? Okay."

I start to tell Paula that I don't know if I want any boy element in my life. But the only thing I do is shake my head and smile. Then I laugh. I can't keep from *not* laughing.

It feels okay. It feels even better than that.

Paula, I'm so lucky to have you. You're my girl!

Aaron
Aaron James
Aaron Thurgood James
He's very friendly, polite
He's taller than me and on the skinny side
maybe he should get into bench presses
He really <u>does</u> look strange when he runs
and maybe he's just a little nerdy

He's on the chess team
like Luce was

He's not hot—
not like Doug Nelson is but he's—
he's cool

He's cuter when he smiles
and when he's not wearing his glasses
He makes good grades in almost everything
Paula says he plays the cello
wonder if that's what he wants to do—
play in an orchestra like my dad

he doesn't have a car
wonder if that would make Mama like him more than Lester

not that I care

❧ 15 ❧

WE'RE FINISHING SUNDAY BRUNCH WHEN THE doorbell rings. When I get to the door, I see the hair and automatically know who's there.

Mahri.

I push open the door and give her a hug. "Hey, girl. I'm so glad you came by."

"I hope it's okay."

"It's better than okay. It's great. Come on in."

I want to ask Mahri why it's taken her so long to come over. Why she didn't come after the services like I thought she would. Like all of us thought. But I don't. I can almost feel that she's a little nervous from having my arms around her shoulders while we walk together down the hall. That she might be remembering, like I am, how it was when she and Luce first started going together and he brought her home to meet the family.

It was near the end of the summer. Luce was leaving for

his first year of college in a few weeks. Mama had been a little upset that Luce wasn't going to be there for Sunday brunch.

"Mahri wants me to go with her to a feast, Ma. We'll come here after that."

"Feast? What kind of feast?"

"Ma . . . does it matter? Some people are coming together for a feast, whatever kind it is."

Nobody got anything out of Luce that he didn't want to give. Not even Mama.

Luce and Mahri got to our house after their feast and our brunch. Just like today. Mahri had walked with Luce down the hall to meet the family the same way she's walking with me now.

I wonder what Mama noticed when Mahri first walked into the dining room that first day. How shy she seemed to be? How pretty she was?

The first thing I noticed about Mahri was her hair—long, curly, and shiny dark red. Mahri's pretty, but her hair is beautiful. Maybe Mama noticed the same thing and decided that Luce was hung up on Mahri because of her looks. For a long time she acted like that was her opinion.

Of all of us, Dad had been the friendliest. After he got up to shake Mahri's hand, he insisted she take his chair. "I was just getting ready to heat up my coffee. Why don't I bring you a cup?"

Bibi was sweet to Mahri, too, but she's that way with everybody. She got right up from her chair like Dad had, putting together a little snack plate for Mahri—a cinnamon bun, some grapes, crackers, and a couple slices of cheese.

Mama had been semi-awful. At least that's how it seemed to me. It wasn't that she said anything really terrible or acted totally rude. But she didn't have to do any of that to show how she felt.

She gave Mahri halfway smiles. Kept asking "your family" questions even though Luce had told us about Mahri's parents not being around much or a real part of her life since Mahri was sixteen. How Mahri had pretty much been on her own.

The worst was all the talk Mama did about college. She knew good and well Mahri was working to support herself and had been even while she was finishing high school. Mahri couldn't even think about going away to college.

"I'm sure Luce has been telling you all about Swarthmore. I think he was set on going there the first minute he walked onto the campus. We visited several colleges last summer, but Swarthmore . . ."

On and on she went.

Later I told Luce I was *never* bringing anybody home I really liked. He just laughed. "Mama's okay, Tika. She just wants the best for us. 'Course, sometimes her opinion of what that best *is* ain't even close! But, persevere. In the end, she'll come around."

Mama had come around. Eventually. A little bit more every time Luce came home for his college breaks and brought Mahri over. She didn't even go into a coma when she found out Mahri was almost three years older than Luce. *That* almost threw me.

Mama probably came all the way around when she finally figured out how much Luce cared about Mahri and that nothing *she* could do was going to change his mind.

Now, walking into the dining room with Mahri, it's hard to believe it was ever any other way.

"Mahri!" Mama gets up and puts her arms around Mahri. "I'm so happy to see you. Why didn't you let us know you were coming? You could have joined us for brunch."

She grabs Mahri's hand and pulls her over to the table. "There's still some fruit and muffins. What can I get for you . . . You have to try one of the muffins. . . ."

Dad chuckles as he gets up to hug Mahri; so does Bibi. I think I'm not the only one who recognizes Mama's "comings around."

"Thanks, Mrs. Clair, but I'm not hungry."

Bibi excuses herself to go to her room to take her medicine. The rest of us sit back down at the table. Mama pats the cushion of the chair beside her and asks Mahri to sit there.

It's easy and not easy at the same time to sit there talking with Mahri. Easy because we all care about each other in one way or another and want to talk together. Not easy because all of us know that although we're sitting there like we have many times before, nothing is the way it was. Or ever will be again.

We go back and forth about a lot of little stuff. Like the weather: how it seems to be getting warm one day and then cold the next.

"That's Chicago for you," says Dad who's a little smiley but still doing his robot act for the most part.

I think about school stuff I could bring up that might be interesting. But everything that comes into my head is something I have no intention of mentioning, much less discussing. Not here.

So, Mahri? Did you and Luce talk much about him being adopted?

Mama starts talking about a new play scheduled to open at some theater downtown. "I know you like theater, Mahri. Have you ever seen one of August Wilson's plays?

Maybe we can think about going to this one together?"

It's one of Mama's "let's broaden ourselves" topics. I guess she can't help herself. Even when she's going out of her way to be as friendly as possible.

She seems to be succeeding with Mahri. I see it in both their faces when she leans over to kiss Mahri on the cheek again before she heads to the kitchen to get more ice water.

Mama hasn't tried even to hug me for ages. . . .

It's a big relief when Bibi comes to get Dad so they can go to the den to watch baseball. Then Mama gets a call from her friend in California. I know she's about to settle in for one of their marathon conversations. When Mahri and I carry some plates into the kitchen, Mama waves us away. An "I'll get that later" move. She seems to mean it.

Since this is one of Chicago's good weather days, I ask Mahri to take a walk with me. As soon as we get outside, I lead the way to Bibi's garden. A place where I figure we'll be able to talk.

Mahri has her surprise when we first get there. "This is lovely! I had no idea that a garden this beautiful was here." Then I get a surprise when we start walking around and I hear how much she knows about gardens.

"Ummm. Smell the lavender. And look at all that yellow

columbine! And blue columbine over there in the middle of those hostas."

The flowers she's excited about look like cups with wobbly legs. Flower aliens. But I'm still impressed. "How do you know so much about flowers?" Mahri lives in a high-rise where there's no hope of a garden.

She shrugs. "Because I love them, I guess. Reading about them, dreaming of having a garden someday. I go to the conservatory in Garfield Park every chance I get."

I wonder if Mahri ever talked to Luce about flowers and gardens. If he ever teased her about loving clumps of growing stuff. I wonder, but I don't say anything.

Mahri calls the name of one kind of flower or another the entire time we walk through the garden. It's amazing. "Mahri, you have to come here one day with Bibi. She loves this garden already, but she'll love it even more walking around with you."

I've been looking at the flowers while I'm listening to Mahri. When I look at her after mentioning Bibi, I see tears soaking her cheeks. "Mahri . . ."

She holds up her hand. "Don't, Leah. I'm okay. It's just that it's so . . . so lovely here. Beautiful, peaceful. Spiritual. A real find in the city. Being here I can't keep from thinking about Luce. Even feeling a little closer to him." Mahri holds her face up to the sky and doesn't even lift her hands to wipe away the tears. "He was all those things, too."

I reach for Mahri's hand. It's the best thing I can think of to do.

We decide to take the long way back. By the lake. Even though it's a Sunday and the weather is great, it's not nearly as crowded as it normally would be. After we walk there for a few minutes, I finally get my courage together to bring up what I hadn't been able to in the garden.

"Mahri, did Luce ever say anything to you about his birth parents? You know, wondering who they were? Maybe wanting to get to know them?"

Mahri stops and looks out at the lake. Today it's like a pale blue mirror. After she doesn't say anything right away, I wonder if she's trying to remember or to decide what to tell me. Then she looks at me and answers. "Luce never talked much about being adopted. At least not to me. I don't think that's the way he usually thought of himself."

"I don't think of him that way either, Mahri, I just—"

Mahri catches my arm. "No. Leah, I know you don't. That's not what I'm trying to say." She links her arm in mine and starts walking again. "What I mean is that I probably brought it up more than he did. Like once asking him if he ever thought about finding his birth parents."

I hold my breath waiting for what Mahri will say next.

"He said he already knew the most important thing about them: that they gave him up so he could have a better life than the one they could give him. He said he was glad they made that decision because there were other choices they could have made that wouldn't have been as good."

I feel heat in my chest and behind my eyes, almost able to hear my brother speaking those words.

Mahri stops again and looks at me. "And he said he hoped they—his birth parents—were as happy as he was." A smile spreads across her pretty face. "It's like I said, Leah: Luce was like that garden—beautiful, peaceful. Spiritual. A real find in this city."

Mahri laces her fingers through mine. I wish I could hold my wet face up to the sun like she does, but I can't. I keep it down and my eyes on the curvy sidewalk of the lake path. The question I decide *not* to ask stays quiet in my head.

Do you think Luce would mind me trying to find out if they are?

❧ 16 ☙

THIS WAS A BAD IDEA. A TERRIBLE IDEA.

I sit there on the steps of the school wondering what in the world possessed me to tell Paula it would be okay for her to ask Aaron James to get together with the two of us after school.

He probably changed his mind about coming.

I try not to pull at my hair or pick my nails or move my leg back and forth.

So what if he did. I don't care.

I fail at everything I'm trying not to do. And I'm so busy trying *not* to do anything but sit there and be cool that I don't see Paula and Aaron until they are almost right in front of me. I get up too fast and almost trip over my own feet.

"Hey, girl." Paula doesn't give me a look so I guess I haven't made too big a fool of myself.

"Hi, Leah." Aaron reaches for my hand like he's getting

ready to shake it. Then he pulls it back before I can do anything.

He's nervous, too.

I relax a little and smile. "I was beginning to wonder
where you guys were."

"It's my fault we're late. Sorry." Aaron smiles. Or tries to.

"Yeah, Mr. Board One here of the chess team had to meet
with the lesser boards."

Paula gives Aaron a thumbs-up sign. He grins. Finally.

"Congratulations, Aaron. That's great." I remember Luce
playing Board One when he was on the chess team, but I
don't mention it.

"Hey, we'd better get started. The El waits for no one."
Paula's grinning like she's performed magic or something. I
ignore her and grab my roller pack.

The sidewalks are wide enough for the three of us to walk
side by side, but Paula somehow manages not to fit. I cut
my eyes at her as she trails behind. We both know what
she's doing.

We walk like that for a minute, nobody saying anything.
Then I hear Paula's voice directly behind me.

"So, how'd the rest of your day go, Leah? You know, after
junior English prep when I saw you?"

"Okay. How about yours?"

"Great. How about yours, Aaron?"

"Okay, I guess."

For a minute I wonder if it's going to be like this all the way to the El stop. Paula yelling at the two of us from behind, and Aaron and I staring straight ahead, answering her back.

This was a great *idea, Paula. Yeah. Right.*

I'm about to stop walking and *make* Paula fall into step with us when Aaron starts. "Leah, ah—" He cuts himself off to clear his throat. Then he starts again. "Speaking of junior English prep, have you decided, um, what you're going to write your report about? You know, the one that'll be passed on to the English teacher you get next year?"

I think I'm starting to say I haven't. But at that same moment, I get a picture in my mind of Paula and me whispering how we'd like to do a report about that ridiculous toupee Mr. Williams insists on wearing and then getting so tickled we almost break up sitting right there in class in front of him. Maybe it's the combination of the two that does it, but whatever it is makes a chuckle-snort fly out of my mouth before I can stop it. Something like "*kchmffffffsss.*"

"Now, *that* sounds like a great topic!"

Geez. Is he making fun of me?

My head jerks around. Aaron's face is right in front of me.

I see his smile—a real one. And his twinkling eyes. The only thing I can do is smile back. Then laugh, right along with him. "Yeah, a whole lot more interesting than what I'll probably end up choosing."

From then on it's easy. I walk alongside Aaron while we talk about regular stuff. I stop paying attention to Paula, who isn't trailing behind us anymore but almost a half block ahead!

When we get to the sports store where Paula has stopped, as usual, she insists she just *has* to go inside to check on something she ordered. I don't believe her, but it doesn't matter.

Paula heads for the door of the store while Aaron and I stand there. For a second I panic again and wonder if it would be better to follow Paula in. Then I decide just to check out everything in the purple display window. *Every* single thing.

Now that we've stopped he might not have anything to say. What should I *start talking about?*

Through the reflections in the window I see that Aaron has turned to look at me. Then, right after the door closes behind a couple that followed Paula into the store, he gets right to the point. "Leah, there's a play I'd like to take you to . . ."

I turn to look at him. He's taken his glasses off and I get

a better look at his eyes. They're beautiful. Light brown. Like amber.

"... *A Midsummer Night's Dream*. I studied it in eighth grade but have never seen it. Do you ... ah, do you like Shakespeare?"

I don't think before I answer. "I'm not sure."

His eyes get me distracted and I don't finish everything I started to say. I'm tempted to turn back around and look at him through his reflection in the display window, but I keep on without doing that. "I mean, when I was a freshman and complained to ... to my brother about how hard it was to read *Julius Caesar*, he said he only started liking Shakespeare after he got to see one of the plays."

It crosses my mind that I just said something about Luce and kept talking. I keep going faster. "I've never seen any of his plays. That's why I don't really know if I like Shakespeare or not."

"Will you go with me and find out? The tickets are for a Saturday afternoon. Three weeks from now." Aaron's amber eyes smile along with his lips. I smile back automatically.

I wonder how he happens to have tickets. If he goes to plays ... like, regularly. But I don't ask anything.

"I'd like to go. I'll have to check with my parents, but yes, that'll be great."

I'm surprised how easy what I'm saying comes out. And how almost natural it feels.

"Great."

Now Aaron turns to look into the display window. "Ah, I don't have a car, so my sister will drop us off and pick us up. I hope that's okay."

That's better than okay. Having a car is no big deal in my book.

I turn back to the window and answer his reflection. "No problem."

Then for no reason in particular, both of us grin. He's looking at my reflection in the display window and I'm looking at his. I have no idea what he's thinking about and am glad he can't read my mind.

Well, Mama. Let's see what kind of objections you will raise about Aaron James. He's taking me to see Shakespeare and his sister—not him*—will be driving the car. How about that!*

❧ 17 ❧

BIBI'S PLANTING LATE THIS YEAR. SHE SAYS THAT IN Chicago it's better to plant after May fifteenth because there's probably not going to be any more frost after then. Now it's after the fifteenth of June. School will be out next week.

Bibi asks me to help her with the planting. I'm in such a good mood, I say okay without even thinking. When I get outside, the warm air makes my mood even better. I start teasing around without even realizing it.

"Bibi, you should think about growing something besides these same old flowers. Maybe something like . . . hmmm, like hostas. You know, perennials. And hostas would grow good even in the shade of this little triangle patch."

Bibi's eyes get wide like I knew they would. She straightens up to stare at me over her flat of impatiens. "Well, listen to you! Just when did *you* become Miss Garden Lady?"

I smile to myself, thinking how Mahri had loaned me a

book about perennials. I hadn't actually asked her for it; she insisted that I borrow it when I saw it in the back of her car the day she took me home after we ran into each other at 57th Street Books. I'd feel a little guilty if I didn't read at least some of it.

I don't mention any of this to Bibi. "See? You didn't think I was listening those times we walked in the garden. Un-huh, I know. I been telling you, Bibi. This still water right in front of you runs deep!"

Bibi shakes her head and laughs. "Must be that young man—the one who's been calling here almost every day these last couple of weeks. Young Mr. Aaron. He must be a plant person."

I look down at the rows of baby flowers in the flat so Bibi won't see me smiling. "Shame on you, Bibi. Accusing me of getting to know about something because of a boy. Um um *um*! You *got* to know better!"

It feels good to tease and laugh with Bibi. Sometimes I still get a little uncomfortable even wanting to laugh, much less feeling like I'm in a good mood. But never with my grandmother. And especially not today. A beautiful, almost-summer Saturday.

My first-date-with-Aaron day!

So far both Mama and Dad seem okay about me going

out with Aaron. I brought it up after dinner one night when both of them were together. Dad didn't say much of anything, as usual, but he acted like he liked the idea.

Dad wants me to be happy.

Mama didn't say much either. Probably because I said the part about Aaron taking me to see *A Midsummer Night's Dream* first. She didn't attack with her usual who-what-where-when questions, but she probably will before I leave. Like she always did with Luce. He'd be almost out the door and there Mama would be with more of *the* questions. "Now, it's just you and Angelle, right? And just the movies or will you be going somewhere afterward?" She already knew the answers to most of what she asked, but that never stopped her from asking again. And again.

No matter what, nothing *Mama dreams up is going to wreck this date.*

When I look back at Bibi, she's still smiling at me. "You like this young man, don't you."

"Yep, I do. He's . . . he's special."

Bibi makes a row of V-shaped holes in the dirt. "Tell me how."

A collection of Aaron pictures moves through my head. The ones I've memorized from sitting with him and Paula in the lunchroom. From talking to him on the phone and going together to the El station after school on Tuesdays and Fridays when neither of us has anything to do. I see the gold-brown eyes. The smile that's serious and something else at the same time. The voice that's mostly deep. Except when he's talking about something he's super-interested in and excited about. Like a chess match.

I decide what I want Bibi to know. "Well, for one thing, he's cool in a way some guys aren't. Like with who he is. You know, like being smart. Making terrific grades doesn't freak him out. He likes Shakespeare and doesn't care who knows it."

While I'm handing Bibi a bunch of violet impatiens roots, one for each of her little holes, I grin, thinking about a word I might have used several weeks ago to describe Aaron. "You know what he'd probably say if people want to call him a nerd? He'd say, 'That's *their* problem!'"

"I'm looking forward to meeting this Aaron. He sounds like my kind of guy." Bibi rests back on her legs before beginning another row of holes. "You know, hearing you right now, I'm remembering the first time your mother talked to me about your father. She was all smiles just like you, talking about this 'fine young man' in her psychology class. Soon after that it was Simon this, Simon that, Simon, Simon, Simon. And before I knew it, Simon was in the family."

I have to stop myself from rubbing my hands on my knees to brush away dried dirt. "Come on, Bibi, quit it. It's just one date. And you haven't heard me doing a bit of Aaron this-ing and that-ing."

Bibi chuckles while she goes back to her digging. "But I think I'm going to."

I get more flowers out of the flat for Bibi, curious about what she said about my parents. "How long did Mama and Dad go together before they got married?"

"Let's see." Bibi sits back on her legs again. "It was Lexie's sophomore year in college when they met, and they married two months after she graduated. So, a little over two years."

Once I heard Mama talking to Luce about her and Dad dating. She's never said anything to me.

Bibi bends over to pat more dirt around the flowers she's already planted. "From the time they were little, both my daughters seemed set on what they wanted to be when they grew up. Your auntie Ingrid, dragging around her little bag of Legos, determined to be an architect. And sure enough, that's what she is today. And then there was your mother, forever tiptoeing her way through the house, equally as determined to be a dancer. Said she wanted to dance on Broadway. Then along came Simon. After that it seemed to be all about being married to him."

Bibi gets ready to stand up. I hold out my hand for support and she catches onto it. "For a while—over three years—it looked like children weren't going to be a part of the Simon-Lexie picture. Then came that wonderful day at the agency, Rock-A-Bye I think it was called. And, of course, a few years later . . ."

I don't hear anything else Bibi says.

An agency . . . ?

Rock-A-Bye . . . ?

Rock-A-Bye Agency.

An adoption agency!

I stand up beside Bibi and hope she hasn't been watching my face and seeing my eyes and mouth get wider and wider. Then I tell her I have to run into the house for a minute while I'm already on my way.

This day is turning out to be even greater than I've imagined!

❧ 18 ☙

First I think of heading to Dad's laptop, but remember that he's in his little office, working on it. Then it occurs to me that it will be easier to just use the phone book. I go right to the kitchen cupboard, open the fat drawer at the top, pull out the telephone book, take it to the counter, and turn to the R's.

Roche . . .

Rochelle . . .

Rock . . .

Rock-A-World . . .

Rocker . . .

There's no listing for "Rock-A-Bye." I slam the phone book shut.

Shoot!

I wonder if I should look for it in the Yellow Pages and remember that Dad has been looking for that directory for weeks. He still swears that Mama tossed it because it was cluttering up her cupboard book space.

Then I got another thought.

Maybe Rock-A-Bye is in one of the suburbs.

I think maybe Bibi might walk in on me if I use the phone in the kitchen to call directory assistance. I told her I'd be back in a minute, but she still might decide to come inside. I want to make sure nobody walks in on me. Since Dad's still in his office and Mama's out with one of her friends, I head to their bedroom to use the phone there.

I pick up the receiver and punch in four-one-one. The operator answers after two rings.

"City and state please."

"Ah . . ."

"Hello? City and state please."

"Illinois . . . ah, I mean, I don't know the city, but Illinois is the state."

"Yes?"

"Could you . . . I mean, please see if you have a listing called Rock-A-Bye."

"I beg your pardon?"

"Rock-A-Bye. It's a place, but I don't know exactly what city it's in."

"One moment please."

I feel myself holding my breath.

"Please hold for the number."

"Wait! I want to know where . . ."

Before I can get it out that I want to know the address and not particularly the telephone number, the automatic message comes on.

"Thank you for calling. The number, 847-555-1376, can immediately be connected for no additional charge if you press one now."

I automatically press one. Then I panic!

What did I do that *for? I don't want to talk to anybody there. I just want to know where it is. What am I going to s—*

"Good afternoon, Rock-A-Bye. How may I help you?"

I almost hang up when someone answers the phone. Then a choking sound comes out sounding like a word.

"*Caahhh* . . ."

I'm about to move the phone away from my mouth when I hear myself say actual real words. I push it closer to my ear and mouth.

"Yes, you can help me. I have an appointment there tomorrow morning, but I've misplaced the address. Would you please give it to me again?"

"Certainly. Rock-A-Bye is located at . . ."

I start smiling while I listen. Then it turns into a grin. I don't know if it's because I'm proud of myself for taking

care of business like a pro or actually having the information I was trying to get. But it doesn't matter.

I know where they got Luce!

I almost can't wait to tell Paula, but I know I have to. I
want to give her this news in person and don't have time
now. First I have to finish with Bibi in the garden. Then I
have to get ready to see Shakespeare for the first time.

I hang up and head back to the kitchen. But a strange
sound I hear makes me stop on the way.

❦ 19 ❦

THE SOUND IS COMING FROM THE LITTLE ROOM ON the other side of the dining room. Dad's office. I peek in and see him sitting in front of his laptop. But instead of working on it, he's playing his flute. The wooden one with lots of fancy decorations he and Mama got when they went to New Mexico the time Dad's orchestra gave a concert there. He says the flute is an authentic instrument. Like ones created by the First Americans.

I've never heard Dad play that flute before. Or even seen him hold it. Ever since he brought it home, I've only seen it lying on one of the shelves of the built-in bookcase in his office.

Wonder what made him decide to play it now?

The flute makes long, empty sounds. Like the sound of the recorders we used to play in grade school. The music sounds better than what we played, but still a little strange. So is the tune Dad's playing. Not all that bad, but strange. And so sad.

But at least he's doing something besides staring into space. Maybe this is a sign. Maybe this is a good time to have a little talk with Dad.

I want to go in but remember something I need to do first. I head back to the kitchen and look out the back door. My grandmother's still on her knees in her garden, even though all of the flowers seem to be planted. No impatiens are left in the flat.

I step out on the porch. "Hey, Bibi, what are you doing? I don't see any more places to plant."

Bibi keeps poking around without looking up. "I'm looking for bugs. Want to help?"

I make a gagging sound. "Definitely *not*. The bug garden is all yours."

Bibi laughs. "I'm looking to dig a few up, not plant them."

"Seriously, Bibi, are you finished with everything I can help you do?"

"All finished, baby. You go on and do whatever you've got planned." She looks up at me and grins. "Like get ready for that big date."

I blow her a kiss as I turn around to leave. "See you later, Beebs."

✿ ✿ ✿

The strange little tune is still floating through the house, slowing me down as I get closer to Dad's office. When I get there and stick my head in so Dad can see me, it stops.

"Hey, Dad." I walk in. "Don't stop. I didn't mean to disturb you."

He puts his flute down. On top of the keyboard of his laptop, which isn't turned on. I wonder if it has been all day.

"You didn't. I was just . . . just messing around with a little tune that keeps going through my head."

It's a pretty sad one, Pops. But you probably already know that.

I walk farther into the room. Dad's office that's more like a mini-office. It's the smallest room in our apartment. And the junkiest. He and Mama argue about it all the time. How Dad never puts anything away, just lays stuff down wherever he happens to be when he's through with it. And how he shoves stuff into a drawer to get it out of sight but then messes up a bunch of other drawers, digging through them trying to find whatever it was.

Dad doesn't let the complaining bother him. Or make him do anything different. "What you see is part of my special filing system," he'll insist. "The in-sight items have a higher priority than the shoved. When you understand it, everything is reasonable and logical."

From the look of the office, practically all of Dad's stuff

has a very high priority. The walls have the only spaces left and even they're getting crowded.

Dad loves art. Especially anything to do with music. A huge poster of Duke Ellington playing the piano and Louis Armstrong on the trumpet takes up almost one whole wall. Dad says it's a joy just to imagine what people heard in that room. "Now, *that* was a jam session." Filling up the space by the window is a funny sketch of Dad dressed in the tails he wears for his concerts, looking like he's struggling to get the music right on his clarinet. A guest soloist Dad knew when they both were in music school drew it. "Simon was sweating it out on stage right while I sweated it out up there on the left."

My favorite thing hanging in the room isn't any kind of picture but a framed poem. One of Mama's friends found it in a book she had and copied the poem in calligraphy. She gave it to my parents on Luce's first Christmas.

I walk over to it now.

I did not plant you.
True.
But when the season is done—
When the alternate prayers for sun and rain
Are counted,

When the pain of weeding and the pride of watching
Are through . . .

I don't hear Dad get up from the chair but can feel him behind me. I can also feel that he's reading the poem over in his mind the same way I am.

. . . then I will hold you high.
A shining sheaf above the thousand seeds grown wild.
Not my planting, but my heaven, my harvest—
My own child.

"Beautiful, isn't it."

"Mmmm." I can tell from his voice that I don't want to turn around to look at Dad. I already know what I'll see.

I should have stopped at the Ellington poster and stared at it.

But I still think this is a perfect time to try to get the information I want. I take a deep breath. "Dad, I was wondering—" I don't get a chance to finish.

"You know, I once thought that telling Luce he was adopted was going to be the hardest thing we would ever have to do." Dad goes on like he didn't even hear me starting to say something. When he moves beside me, I can see the tears on his cheeks out of the corner of my eye.

Oh Dad . . .

"Lexie thought we should do it as soon as Luce was able to understand the concept. You know, the nature-versus-nurture mother thing. Not in those words, of course. But she said it was important to have him hear about it from us—one of us, at least—before he heard it somewhere else. And she was right. Some people can be extremely thoughtless."

You got that *right! Even so-called friends.*

I turn to look at Dad but don't say anything. Even though he's really stuck in being so sad, somehow I want him to go on.

He does. "It turned out that Luce actually loved the story I told him. He would ask to hear it again and again. How I had gone to this place where they kept the most special babies in the world and asked to hold the most special baby of them all."

Dad's voice makes a small choking sound, but he keeps on. "I explained how they put this sweet baby boy into my arms and how I laid one finger in the baby's open hand. How the baby squeezed that finger to say, 'Hey, Dad. I'm your little boy.'"

The tears are pouring down my cheeks now, too. Dad must see them like I saw his. But it's okay. I don't try to wipe mine away like he hasn't either. I just wait for him to go on.

"He was a wonderful harvest, our Luce was, eh, Leah?" Dad links his arm through mine. "A truly wonderful harvest."

I rest my head against Dad's shoulder. "Like no other."

Dad pulls me closer. "Except for his little sister. His beloved Tika. She is also our wonderful harvest. And one we had also the honor to plant."

I wish Dad could pick me up. Hold me up high and then cradle me in his arms like he did when I was little and mostly could see only his knees. At the very least I want to bury my head in his shoulder and have him tell me everything is going to be all right.

But at the same time I want to cradle Dad in my arms. Tell him not to worry because I'm going to love him *double* forever.

But I don't do any of that. I just stand there beside my father in his messy little room, realizing that the most perfect time and the most unperfect time can exist at the same moment.

✺ 20 ✺

IT'S LIKE MY HANDS FREEZE IN THE AIR ABOVE MY
head when I hear Mama's footsteps coming down the hall
toward my room. At least that's where it sounds like they're
headed. But when they stop outside Bibi's door and I hear
Mama start talking to my grandmother, my fingers push at
my hair again, trying to get it back to the way it was just a
minute ago.

I should have left well enough alone.

Once when I was finishing up my hair, my hand accidentally knocked against and wrecked a little ponytail I
had arranged to one side. I had gotten up really early that
morning to finish typing the last part of a book report.
Maybe that's why after I wrecked my ponytail, my hand
automatically reached up to hit an invisible Delete key I
must have imagined above my head. I had been at the
computer so long, I started thinking that I could punch
a key to erase my mistake, even a lopsided hairdo.

I stare at myself in the mirror above my dresser and decide I really *should* leave well enough alone. I shouldn't exchange the gold barrette pinning my hair behind one ear with the silver one that Aunt Monique sent me from Mexico. Gold looks better with yellow than silver. I shouldn't change into my jean skirt even though it makes me look better from behind. The black skirt is more appropriate for a play. I think.

You look okay, Leah. Even better than that.

I know I'm going to make myself crazy if I keep looking so I turn away from the mirror.

Just go on, get it over with. Go past the judge and get the verdict.

I don't see Mama when I step out into the hall but hear her and Bibi talking in Bibi's room. Since my shoes hardly click at all on the wood floors, I think for a second about slithering against the wall to make it past Bibi's room without either of them seeing me. But my shoes must have made more of a noise than I thought.

"Leah, is that you?"

Bibi's eagle ears at work.

"Yep, it's me."

"Finally. Well, come on in and let's see."

I walk into Bibi's room. She's in her chair, facing the door. Mama's on Bibi's bed with her back to the door.

A big grin breaks out on Bibi's face. "You look lovely, baby. Doesn't she, Lexie?"

Okay. Here it comes.

Mama turns around. Partly. Mostly just her head. She looks at me over her shoulder. I wait for her to finish turning, but she doesn't.

"Ummmm," she says. Then, "Yes."

What?

I automatically move farther into Bibi's room. Like I want to make *sure* Mama sees me. All of me. Everything. My hair pinned to one side with the gold butterfly barrette she gave me my first day of high school.

"I guess this is symbolic recognition of your really leaving the nest."

I move even farther. Mama can absolutely see it all now. My black skirt that almost reaches the floor. My feet in the new shoes she doesn't even know I bought. Paula has a pair exactly like them. We bought them together the day the new shoe store opened on Fifty-third Street.

"Those shoes look great, Leah." Bibi still has this big grin on her face. "Gracious me. How I wish I could still wear shoes with so little leather. Just those tiny straps."

Mama looks down at my feet. Kind of. She smiles. Kind of.

I'm almost in the middle of Bibi's room, standing completely still.

"You're a vision, sweetheart. Isn't she, Lexie."

Mama can see all of me now without turning her head at all. She looks at me with a half smile and nods her head. "Ummmm," she says again.

Forget this!

"Thanks, Beebs. Ah, I forgot something in my room. Excuse me a sec."

I get out of there as fast as I can. The *click-click* of my new thin-strap shoes sounds a little like tiny bullets hitting against wood somewhere far in the distance.

Not ONE question
no why-are-you-wearing-that
Not even a why-don't-you-put-your-hair suggestion
My hair's not pulled up, Mama
it's mostly hanging around my face
the way you say it looks best
Did you even notice?
Did you notice ANYTHING?

You used to care. I think you did. But maybe
it just seemed that way because of Luce.

Remember how you always said something to Luce about
how he looked before he went out on a date? Always?
ALWAYS!
Of course Luce always looked beautiful.
Even when he put those gross yellow streaks in his
hair that time
But Luce was truly beautiful
inside and out

Maybe you're disappointed that your natural child
is ordinary
not beautiful like your adopted one?

stop stop stop STOP!!
Even thinking that is sick.

but she might not be able to help herself
especially now

❧ 21 ❧

AFTER I BUZZ AARON INTO THE BUILDING, I RUSH TO get to our front door before anybody else can. I look through the peephole and see him standing in the vestibule with someone who has to be his sister. I open the door. "Hi."

Aaron gives me a huge smile. His eyes twinkle. I stand back and pull our door open wider. "Come on in."

The girl is tall like Aaron and has the same amber eyes. I can tell just from the way she's standing that she's probably like him in a lot of ways. Straightforward. Very sure of herself. Before he can say anything, she comes up to me and introduces herself. "You must be Leah. Hi, I'm Rita, Aaron's sister."

"I know." I think that sounds dumb since we've never met. "I mean, I figured you were. You look like Aaron."

Rita grins. "Actually, Aaron looks like me. But it doesn't matter because I'm better known as Aaron's driver."

At that second I want to say, "Okay, Aaron's driver, let's get on the road!" but I know I can't.

I look at Aaron and lead the way to the living room. "I'm ready, but my parents want to meet you before we go."

Dad is sitting on the piano bench, holding his clarinet. He actually had been playing along with one of his CDs. It's the first time he's done that in ages. He stopped only when he heard the doorbell.

"Dad, this is Aaron James and his sister Rita."

The three of them say hello to one another. Dad gets up to shake their hands. I look around the corner of the entrance to the living room to see if Mama and Bibi are coming down the hall.

Please hurry so we can get this over with!

"Mr. Clair, I've seen you playing in the orchestra." Aaron's amber eyes seem to be sparkling more than ever. "I've never actually heard you, but that's probably a good thing since you weren't playing a solo."

Dad laughs. It seems real. "That's a *very* good thing!" He smiles at Aaron. "Leah tells me you play an instrument. The cello."

"Yes sir. I love the cello, but so far I'm a much better listener than player. The best playing I do is putting on a Yo-Yo Ma CD."

Dad's real-for-sure laugh rings through the room and I know we're having the same memory.

Being a musician, Dad insisted that both Luce and I take music lessons. I took piano and learned to play okay, I guess. Sometimes when he asks me, I play piano-clarinet duets with Dad.

Luce said playing the piano was too ordinary and decided to take violin. He was terrible. He said he really tried but had no talent. One time Dad found him practicing in the bathroom with the shower running. Luce said the water helped drown out the sound, making it better for him and anybody who might be listening. "Face the facts, Dad. My best violin playing is going to be putting on a Regina Carter CD."

Dad's still smiling when he puts his hand on Aaron's shoulder. "My son said something similar about playing the violin. But I have a feeling there's as much modesty in your statement as there was truth in his."

Dad's look at Aaron goes a lot deeper than the smile. One reason is probably because he sees how Aaron has been gazing at the chess set on the coffee table. The heavy marble board with the jade playing pieces. It was Luce's favorite. He got it for his sixteenth birthday. I almost pray that neither of them will get started on chess. That they won't even mention it.

I'm glad when Mama comes into the living room. She stops beside me.

"Mama, this is Aaron and his sister Rita."

More hello's and hand shaking. I look down the hall to see if Bibi's coming. Mama sees me.

"My mother was hoping to join us." She smiles at Aaron. "To meet you. But she got a long-distance phone call from my sister, who's actually in Ecuador on business."

In a way I'm sorry and glad at the same time that Bibi's busy. Now it won't look so much like we're ganging up on the James family.

I'm almost holding my breath, waiting to see what else Mama's going to say.

Here it comes. What she really *thinks.*

I stand there waiting for what will come next, but Mama doesn't say anything. Nothing. It's almost . . . no. It *is* weird.

I want to leave. "Ummmm, we should probably get started. The play starts at four o'clock."

I've started moving toward the door when the question finally comes. "Will you be going to the play also, Rita?" But it's Dad who's asking.

"No sir. I'm just the chauffeur."

"Will you be picking them up?"

"Yes. Aaron has a cell phone. He'll call when they're ready."

"I thought we'd get a little something to eat after the play, Mr. Clair. If that's okay."

"That's fine, Aaron. I'm just making sure you have a way back."

"Thanks, Dad. Thanks—" I'm about to thank Mama, too, when I realize it would sound strange.

For what? For not *saying anything?*

I hear the choruses of "nice to meet you" and "have fun" behind me and let out a big breath when all three of us get to the door.

When I turn around to wave good-bye, Dad has his arm around Mama's shoulders. "Have fun, you two." His smile is like his laugh was. Real.

Mama's smiling, too. But she seems to be sending it more to Dad than to me.

Figures. She's not even caring that I'm going out.

The door clicks shut behind us. When I hear it, I begin to realize that something's missing. I don't know what until I get settled in the front seat and hear the snap of the car door when Aaron shuts it tight.

Mama didn't say, "Be careful!"

I can't remember a single time when she didn't say that to Luce when he was leaving to go somewhere. And while we're driving out of our park onto Fifty-fourth Street, I'm trying to, really, really hard.

✻ 22 ✻

RITA DROPS US DOWN THE STREET FROM THE ENTRANCE to Navy Pier. Where the theater is. She tells us she'll pick us up in this same spot. Then she drives off, waving good-bye by wiggling her fingers over the top of her head.

The pier isn't packed with people the way it usually is on weekends. Especially one like this. There's not a cloud in the sky and the air is actually . . . well, soft. Soft and warm. It all seems perfect. Maybe that's why I notice right away that I've gotten nervous. So much so that I almost can't walk. It's taking everything I can do just to step up onto the sidewalk and walk away from the edge of the curb.

Suddenly a whole collection of feelings starts washing over me like they've been mixed into a pitcher of cold water being drizzled over my head. They come slowly at first but get faster and harder.

I shouldn't be doing this.

Not going out. Not with a boy. Any boy. Not on a date.

Why did I even think about doing this?

What made me think it would be okay?

I must want *terrible horrible awful things to happen because they do when . . .*

I get dizzy. Almost like I'm about to throw up. "Aaron, I . . ."

I feel Aaron's hand on my back. It's the gentlest of pressure, but it forces me in the direction of a bench at the edge of the grass by the walk leading to the entrance of the pier. "There, Leah. Let's go over there."

I can't say, "That's okay, I'm fine," or keep myself from moving with him to the bench. When we get there, I sit down automatically. Then the worst happens. The cold-water pitcher above me turns into a hot-water faucet inside me. It lets loose with an awful flood of tears. They start pouring down my cheeks and onto my new yellow short-sleeve linen blouse that took me almost two hours to pick out to wear.

"Better?" Aaron's voice is so soft.

"Better." I'm telling the truth.

The handkerchief he gave me is sopping wet in my fist. It's embarrassing, like everything else has been ever since we stepped out of Rita's car. I can't even make myself look at

Aaron. "I'll give you back your handkerchief after I wash it."

"No problem."

We sit there, not saying anything. Somehow I know it's okay with Aaron that we are. Maybe because of the way he's sitting there. Still, quiet. So calm. I begin to feel the same way.

After another minute I look down at Aaron's handkerchief. A strange, funny thought hits me.

"Do you always carry a handkerchief? I mean . . . ah . . ."

"You mean it's an old-man thing, having a handkerchief on you. Right?"

I have to chuckle. "Yeah. Kind of."

"Rita says I'm a walking reincarnation of our ancient ancestors." Aaron turns to look at me. "I like to think of it as practical. Being prepared."

He leans forward, resting his elbows on his knees but still looking at me. "I should also probably tell you this about me. I keep a small notebook and two ballpoint pens in one of my pockets all the time. A fold-up umbrella stays in my backpack. And I *always* have a handkerchief on me." His grin shows two rows of straight, white teeth.

I smile but then look down at my hands. I'm feeling better—much better—but still so embarrassed I don't have any idea of what to say. "Aaron, I . . ."

He rests against the back of the bench and folds his hands in his lap. "Excuse me, Leah, but there's something else I want you to know about me." He turns to look at the city skyline that fills in the edge of the lakefront. A sky-wide painting.

"If I lost my sister the way you lost Luce . . . if I lost Rita . . . well, there's no way in the world to be prepared for that. I don't think I could take it. I think the fact that you're handling it at all . . . well, it's amazing. Honest. Just amazing."

Aaron turns back around to look at me. I don't turn away. I don't even want to. Not even when I feel my face wetting up again or watch the big, beautiful circles of amber in Aaron's face cloud over with his own tears.

I stop caring that we keep sitting there and might miss the beginning of the play if we don't get up soon. I don't even mind that people passing by might notice us and our waterworks and think we're strange.

There's only one thing that matters. I begin to know somewhere deep inside of me that I would give anything on this earth to be able to hug my brother again. I would hug him tighter than anyone has ever been hugged in the history of humankind.

I don't really think you care, Mama, but in case you do—

We didn't make it to the Shakespeare play but not on purpose. It just turned out that way. The play had started by the time we got to the theater so we walked up and down the pier. Looking. Talking. Laughing. Yep. Laughing for real.

We did get something to eat like Aaron said we were going to. After we saw people coming out of the theater we stopped just like we would have done if we had gone to the play.

We ate outside at a place with candles on the tables. It was so cool. But we hardly ate for talking.

One more thing. We will see a Shakespeare play. Maybe not A Midsummer Night's Dream, but something. Aaron's family has season's tickets. He'll tell the people at the theater they were out of town and couldn't use the tickets that day so he can get tickets for another Saturday. We'll have to take any available seats, but that'll be okay.

When we go we're going to pretend to be going someplace else. We don't want anybody to think we're hung up on Shakespeare.

Sneaking out to see Shakespeare! Cool, huh, Mama. You might even think so yourself
  if you cared

Yeah, it's cool. But nowhere near as cool as Aaron.

❧ 23 ❧

I'M SO BUSY TRYING TO SPOT AARON, I ALMOST RUN right into Ms. Rice.

"Ms. Rice, I'm sorry. I wasn't watching where I was going."

"That's okay, Leah. No harm done." Ms. Rice has this big grin on her face like most people do today, including me. I guess the last day of school is a great day for everybody—students *and* teachers.

"Need I ask where you're off to?" Ms. Rice nods her head toward the door.

"Not exactly yet. I'm meeting . . . ah, a friend first." I wonder why I don't say Aaron's name, but I don't. "We want to check out something before we leave."

"Let me guess. Hmmm. Could it be the corridor with the yellow stripe? The one next year's juniors will be using?"

Hearing Ms. Rice, it almost sounds silly. Almost. But checking out the corridor where you and your classmates will be in September is practically a school tradition. All the kids do it. That's where most of us meet up to say good-bye before we leave for the summer.

Then it's like Ms. Rice is reading my mind. "It's a great tradition, in my opinion. Especially for those meeting in the green corridor—where you and all the other future seniors will be headed this time *next* year."

"Yep." I stand there, not quite knowing what else to say.

"Well, Leah, I'll wish you a happy summer and let you get on your way."

"Thanks, Ms. Rice."

I turn around, ready to wave at Ms. Rice before I turn the corner. But I don't move. "Ah, Ms. Rice?"

"Yes, Leah?"

I know what it is that I want to say to Ms. Rice. I've said it in my head at least twenty times. Maybe thirty. Every time I've passed her office. Especially when I see her door open. During third period. Her open-door time when you can just drop in if you feel like you need to talk.

I've absolutely felt like I needed to talk. I just haven't been able to decide if I *want* to. Or if I should.

So, Ms. Rice, did my brother ever talk to you about being adopted? About wondering who his birth parents were? Do you think he wanted to find out who they were? Don't you think we should know . . . especially now? Do you see any reason why I shouldn't try to find out?

I know that now's my last chance to talk to Ms. Rice, but I just stand there looking at her while she looks at me. Then she starts toward me. "Is there something you want, Leah."

Yes. In twenty-five words or less, I want you summarize everything you know and think about Luce's being adopted.

I give her the biggest smile I can. "I just want to say I'll hope you'll have a great summer, too, Ms. Rice."

"Okay then. See you in September."

I'm about to turn around and go. But it feels like Ms. Rice still has something she wants to say. I wait.

She looks at me for a second, then reaches into her purse and pulls out a pen. "Leah, would you mind giving me a sheet of paper from your little notebook. Yes, that one."

I tear out a sheet of paper from the notebook on top of my pile of books. All the stuff I hadn't been able to fit in my roller pack yesterday and now have to lug home by hand.

After I give the sheet to Ms. Rice, she scribbles something on it, folds it over, and then hands it back to me. I take it and look at her. She nods, so I open it.

Beverly Rice

773/555-8735

"It's my home phone number. Please feel free to call me

anytime, Leah. I'd love to hear from you, if ever or when-ever you'd like to talk."

I fold the paper and put it in my pocket.

"Thanks, Ms. Rice. That's nice of you."

After we wave to each other, I take a deep breath and smile at the slender back in the tan jacket, making its way to the door.

Thanks, Patchouli.

✤ 24 ✤

"COME ON, PAULA. WHAT HARM CAN IT DO?"

"Probably none, but what *good* can it do?"

"Paula, please . . ."

"Leah, please . . ."

I don't think Paula's being difficult on purpose, but she *is* and I want to tell her so. Especially when this is a time a best friend should be making a special effort to be *easy*!

I feel myself getting angry and wait a couple of seconds before I say anything else into the phone. "Okay, Paula, never mind. If that's the way you feel, no problem."

I hold my breath, almost praying that I haven't pushed too far. The relief when I hear her jump in right away is like a cool breeze.

"Leah. wait. You know how I feel. I *want* to help. You know I do. It's just that . . . well, I don't see how driving to—"

I've just got to convince her.

"Paula, Paula. Listen to me." I make my voice calm. "Look, driving to Rock-A-Bye will let me see the place where my parents actually got Luce. It'll be the beginning of . . . you know, the beginning of this journey. I need you to come with me on this beginning, Paula. You're my best friend, my dearest friend. I need you there to support me."

I stop and hold my breath again, half expecting Paula to say, "Okay, Leah, cut the crap." But when all I hear is breathing on the other end, I know that she's at least thinking about it. I wonder if I should mention that she's being a whole lot harder to convince than Mahri was and then decide that I shouldn't. But then there's silence for such a long time. . . .

"Paula . . . ?"

"Okay, okay. I'll go with you and Mahri."

"Great! Thanks, Paula. I owe you one."

"You owe me a *bunch*, girlfriend." Paula takes a deep breath. "Okay, what time are you leaving? Want me to come over to your—?"

And risk something slipping out to my parents? No way!

I cut Paula off. "Uh-uh. No. Mahri and I will pick you up. About eleven. I'll call you on Mahri's cell when we're close to your house."

"Okay. And Leah?"

Please don't ask me "why" again. Please!

"Yeah?"

"What are you wearing?"

I slap my hand over the mouthpiece, hoping I'm covering up most of the laugh that just flew out. I get a picture in my head of Paula imagining two orphan girls dressed in rags, arriving at a Rock-A-Bye, pretending they want to get adopted.

That would be one way to get information, I guess.

I swallow the chuckle still rumbling in my throat. "Nothing special. Just the usual."

"Okay. See you in a few."

"And, Paula? Like I said, thanks. Thanks a lot."

❧ 25 ❧

I LIKE THE CD MAHRI HAS PLAYING IN HER CAR.
From the cover, I thought it would be like most classical
music. The kind Dad's orchestra plays. It's okay but can get
really boring sometimes. Like listening to math set to
music. Mahri's CD, a piano playing by itself, it's . . .well . . .

"That's interesting music."

"*After the Rain?* Um-hm. Like it?"

"Yeah, I do."

"It's one of my favorite CDs. I never even heard of it until
Luce gave it to me. But then, I didn't know anything about
classical music until I started going with Luce."

"Luce?" I don't even try to keep from sounding shocked.
Luce never listened to anything but rap.

"He took me to the symphony on one of our first dates.
To see your dad playing in the orchestra. I told him he was
trying to impress me." Remembering, Mahri smiles. Her
eyes open wider. "He said I was right, but that he also

wanted me to get used to what I would have to put up with after we got married."

I want to turn around to look at Paula, who's riding in the backseat, but I don't. It doesn't matter, though. I can almost feel her eyes practically digging a hole into the back of my head. I hope Mahri's not watching her through the rearview mirror.

Luce and Mahri talking about getting married! Wonder if Mama knew anything about that?

It occurs to me how everything about this day is turning out to be unexpected. And a little bizarre. It's cloudy and drizzly outside and we're riding along the lake, listening to something called *After the Rain*. It's on a CD Mahri got from my brother who thought hip-hop was the only music on the planet worth listening to. The music is kind of gray-green like the lake and sky.

It's almost like the weather has painted everything to match itself. Including us. Everything we bring up and talk about stays in a safe gray-green zone. Nobody brings up anything that's not safe for us to be talking about. Like even mentioning that we're in the car on a Saturday morning, traveling north where a lot of great malls are but not headed to anyplace even close to a mall. No talk about where we're going or why.

Mahri keeps her car in the lane closest to the lake. "I never thought I would like classical music. But after Luce saw how much I enjoyed the concert, he bought me this CD and a couple of others. One of them has music by a composer called Brahms. I love that one, too. Luce thought Brahms was awesome."

"Luce?" I know Mahri has no reason to lie, but still . . .

This time she sees my shocked face and laughs. "Yeah, it's hard to believe, I know. Hip-hop was his favorite, but Luce liked all kinds of music, even though he mostly listened to rap."

The memory dances in my head. Luce and Dad sitting in the den, listening to one of Luce's hip-hop CDs. Luce bobbing to the beat and Dad complaining. "You need to broaden your horizons, son. There's a wealth of music in this world worthy of your attention."

Luce's laugh. One of the new ones he was trying out. "Aw, come on, Dad. I *know* about the wealth—jazz, that old European stuff, bluegrass, R and B, rock, folk . . . want me to go on?" Another new laugh. "Dad, I think it's *you* who needs some broadening. Rap is some of the new wealth."

Luce continuing to grin and to bob with everything he had.

I almost feel his beat in the rhythm of the rain as it starts coming down harder. When I look away from the sky and see Mahri smile, I think she's remembering like me.

"Luce knew how rap irritated your parents. He said he was trying to get them educated."

Mahri turns up the speed of the windshield wipers and slows down to turn off Lake Shore Drive.

The rain has almost stopped when we get there.

ROCK-A-BYE
ESTABLISHED 1931

We're here.

What on earth was I thinking of?

Why did I want to do this?

I force myself to open my eyes that I shut the second we drove up and to look again at the large stone building. I keep staring while I'm wondering what I had expected. Something like a hospital? A long, gloomy house on a lonesome street?

Luce didn't *come from this place. He came from* our *house!*

The building looks more like a school than anything else. Like one of the buildings on the campus of Luce's college. One of those ancient, heavy stone castlelike monstrosities. Stiff old trees stand at each of the corners. Like guards watching over everything in the yard—the stone benches and tables, the narrow stone walks that lead to the entrances. There are at least four.

The building is three stories high. Lined up and down and across each floor are rows of matching windows. With their even squares of glass trimmed in white, they make neat patterns across the stone.

Would Luce's baby mind have remembered this place?

While Mahri drives around the block, I want to say, "Let's turn around and go home. You were both right. This *isn't* a good idea."

But I don't say anything. I just sit there like a coward without muttering a word.

I almost believe Mahri's read my mind when she doesn't turn into the parking lot next to one of the entrances. But then she pulls into a space on the street. Right across from one of the entrances. The main one. It has a curved opening with layers of stone around it. Like the entrance to a museum. The thick door has old-fashioned brass handles on it, one for knocking and one for pulling the door open.

Mahri turns off the ignition key and the rain music stops. She turns to look at me and I know Paula is doing the same thing from the backseat. Neither of them says,

"Well, what now?" but I hear it anyway. I look across the street and ask myself the same thing.

Then Mahri unbuckles her seat belt and puts her hand on the handle of her door. "Do you guys want to get out and look around or go with me? I'm going inside."

❧ 26 ❧

MAHRI DOESN'T WAIT FOR AN ANSWER. CALMLY, LIKE THIS was her plan all along, she gets out of the car, slams the door shut, and stands on the sidewalk beside the car.

I turn around to look at Paula, who's looking at me. I know she's wondering, "What now?" just like I am.

"Leah, are you . . . ah, what . . . ah, do you . . ."

Paula's saying out loud what I'm feeling inside. I roll down my window and stick out my head. "Mahri, how . . . ah, do you think you should?"

Mahri walks to my side of the car. "Leah, when you asked me to drive us here, you said it would help you just to see where your parents got Luce. I decided you're right. I also think it will help even more to see the inside." She puts her hand on the door handle. "Well?"

"Suppose somebody asks you why you're there? You know, what you want?"

"I'll tell them." Mahri pulls the car door open.

"*What?*" Paula and I say it at the same time.

When Mahri giggles, her dancing eyes practically invite me to relax. "Look, I'm over twenty-one. I'll tell anyone who asks that I'm thinking about adopting a baby and need some information. You won't have to do or say anything. While I'm talking, you can just look around. Isn't that what you want to do?" Mahri tilts her head to one side and smiles. "Now, come on."

No wonder Luce loved you so. . . .

"Okay. Let's go." After I step out of the car, I reach for the catch release on the seat so I can pull the seat forward to let Paula out. She puts her hand over mine to stop me.

"No, Leah. You and Mahri go on. It'll be better if I wait in the car. You know, better for snooping around if you're by yourself."

I want to give her a hug, but I just smile and know she can read my heart.

You're my girl, Paula. In the end you always know how to make it easier.

The heavy door makes a hollow sound when we hit the brass knocker against it. I'm almost expecting somebody like Lurch from the Addams Family to step out and say, "Yes?" But nobody comes and the door sort of swings open. After we step inside, it swings closed behind us.

Weird.

I don't know what I was expecting, but I'm surprised when I get inside Rock-A-Bye. Shiny black-and-white tile floors stretch from the little foyer through the big hall beyond it. A large bowl of flowers is on a large round table in the middle of the hall. If there wasn't a woman sitting at a businesslike desk at one side of the hall, I could imagine I was stepping into someone's home. A pretty rich someone.

"Hello, may I help you?" The woman is looking at Mahri. Mahri starts over to the desk. "Yes. I'm here to get some information. . . ." Mahri looks back at me. I get her silent message.

Stop listening, Leah, and get busy. You're on a mission.

I go into the hall and start to wander around slowly, looking in the direction of the rooms opening off from it. There's nobody around. Nobody calling out to tell me to stop. I get braver and move to the wide curved opening leading to the largest room.

It's a living room filled with couches, chairs, low and high tables, lamps of all sizes . . . a bunch of living room things. The furniture is arranged in little groups like it's waiting for little groups of people who will come in to sit and talk.

Let's see. What kind of baby would you like?

There are draperies at the windows and large rugs on a

shiny wood floor. A fireplace. A baby grand piano. And pictures. So many pictures. They are everywhere—on the walls, on the tables, mixed in with books on the built-in bookshelves.

The pictures pull me to them like they're human-body magnets. Pictures of smiling babies sitting by themselves or posed with adults. Little kids dressed up like they're on their way to a party. Teenage kids making happy funny faces for the camera.

I move from one to the other. Even though I don't say it to myself, I know I'm hoping to spot one specific picture. One special baby. A little boy with dark curly hair, fat cheeks, and an almost-dimple in his chin. A photograph that matches a snapshot Dad keeps in a small frame on his messy desk.

The most special baby of them all . . .

I stare at every picture in the room but don't see it.

Are there pictures like this in every room? Pictures of every baby who's ever been here?

On either side of the fireplace, I see entrances to two smaller rooms. One of them has a door leading outside to a small garden enclosed by other walls of the building. Looking up, I can see part of the two floors above.

What's in all these rooms? Do they keep babies here? Is this

*where they bring the babies to give them away? Do they make
people who want to be parents come here and stay for a little
while so they can check them out? Is this where Mama and
Dad . . .*

The questions pile up in my head. Then they push me
back toward the entrance I came through.

I should go and find out.

I'm about to leave the room when I feel someone behind
me. For a second I panic. Then I see it's Mahri.

"I've gotten answers to all my questions. Have you seen
enough?"

*No way. Not even close. I don't know what's in the other
rooms. Is there a picture of Luce anywhere? Are there really
babies here? If there are, what do the rooms they're in look like?
Does each baby have his own bed? Are there soft blankets and
animal toys in the beds with the babies? Did Luce have stuff
like that while he waited by himself in one of those beds?*

I want to tell Mahri no, but know it wouldn't make any
sense to say that. I nod my head.

On our way to the car, Mahri says they told her that the
first step in adopting is to attend an orientation meeting.
"They invited me to one they're having next Tuesday. It's
probably one way of making sure you're really interested
after you've come here to look around." She holds up some

papers she has in her hand. I hadn't noticed them. "They also gave me this to read. It explains open adoption."

"What kind of adoption?"

"Open adoption." Mahri's looking at one of the sheets. "The kind where birth parents and adoptive parents meet and get to know each other."

I stop in my tracks.

That means Mama and Dad know *who Luce's parents are. Maybe even Luce knew. Maybe all of them know, except me. But why wouldn't they tell me? I have just as much right to know as anybody. I'm Luce's sister!*

I feel myself getting sweaty and it's nowhere near hot.

Maybe they have other children. Maybe Luce has a birth sister! Maybe that's why they didn't tell me.

Mahri is about to cross the street and stops when she realizes I'm not beside her. "Leah? What's wrong?" She stops and looks at me.

"What you said . . . open adoption . . . that means . . ." I sound like a robot whose program has gotten screwed up.

Mahri moves next to me. "Leah, wait." She catches my arm and holds on to it. "Open adoption is their policy these days, but it's only been that way for the last ten years or so. Way after your parents got Luce. Before that adoptions were usually closed. You know, no contact between birth and adopting parents. No knowing who was who."

I can tell from just looking into Mahri's face that she knows what's going through my head. At least some of it. "Okay, Leah?"

I nod my head. "Okay."

I start to ask her if she found out anything else. Not that it matters. Coming here has already helped me much more than I had ever thought it would. It's helped me answer the question I've been asking myself over and over.

Yes, I want to get the facts about Luce. I'm sure I do. I'm absolutely sure!

It's a sign. I'm <u>sure</u> it is! This is something I'm supposed to do!

I didn't even have to look all the way through Dad's junky drawer. The papers were near the top, under some folded copies of clarinet scores and a fat envelope with an expired insurance policy. All of it right there for anybody to see—the adoption placement agreement, the final adoption decree, and the letter from the lawyer saying that everything was final and that the new birth certificate would be sent as soon as it was issued.

Mama would have a fit if she knew such important information was just lying around loose. She probably thinks it's in the safe-deposit box at the bank. She told me once all our important papers are kept there.

Maybe Dad took Luce's papers out of the vault recently—

No matter. Finding that information was a sign sure as anything I could get to tell me to keep on keeping on.

❧ 27 ❧

NOW'S A GOOD TIME. GO IN THERE NOW. OKAY?

Okay.

Well, go on. What are you waiting for? Just open the door the rest of the way and step inside.

Okay, okay. In just a minute.

I'm having this conversation with myself and beginning to think I'm going totally crazy. I stop in the middle of the hallway I've walked up and down at least five times already and give myself one final command.

Just do it!

I have my hand on the doorknob when Mama calls out. "Leah? Is that you?"

Now you have to!

"Yeah, it's me."

And I'm coming in there so you can tell me what I need to know.

I pull the door open all the way and see Mama standing on the stepladder in the middle of a huge mess.

For over two hours before I started patrolling the hallway, Mama had been organizing things in the huge storage closet. We keep all kinds of stuff in there—suitcases, folding tables and chairs, stacks and stacks of Dad's music, golf clubs he hasn't used since I was about six, piles and boxes of photos, the dollhouse Luce and Dad built for me. . . . When Dad or I lose something, we'll ask, "Did you look in the pit?" But only each other. To Mama that long closet with built-in drawers at one end is one of our apartment's greatest features.

"When we first saw this place, Lexie got more excited about that storage space than anything else." Dad always mentions this when Mama shows off the closet to anybody interested in being that nosey. "Not the refinished hardwood floors or the little fireplace in the master bedroom. Not even the fact that the kitchen had been modernized—which sold me! Lexie considered this place a find because of that closet."

It *is* convenient. Like for keeping bikes during warm weather when we use them a lot. It's so much easier to get them from the pit than to go back and forth to our locker in the basement. But it's still just a closet.

Mama's at the top of a stepladder, trying to get to the boxes piled on the top shelf of the closet. "I'm looking for that box of drawings. You know, that special collection. Have you seen it lately?"

Mama's talking about her collection of things Luce and I made. Mostly when we were young and dumb enough to think that everything we brought home was art. She kept drawings and little craft projects and whatever else of ours she decided should be saved. She keeps all of it in a big brown packing box that looks like a lot of the other boxes stacked in the closet. Once when Luce asked her why she was saving that stuff, she said she wanted to have it to show her grandchildren.

I haven't seen the box for ages. And the last time I looked inside, there was mostly only Luce's stuff. His pictures, his plaster of paris handprint, his painted rock paperweights, his little clay figures. Even a plastic pill bottle with his baby teeth.

I've never seen anything *that has* my *baby teeth in it.*

"Leah?" Mama's waiting for an answer.

"Nope. I haven't seen it."

But there's something you might help me *find. Information.*

I look at Mama, standing on her toes so she can push open the tops of the boxes. She can't really see inside them that way so she tries to figure out what's in them by feeling around.

Just say it. Tell her you want to find something, too, and need her help to do it.

Mama pulls at a box behind the one she just closed. The way something inside rattles makes her push it back again. "I don't think your father would have moved it, but then you never know. I remember seeing it not too long ago. In the spring . . ."

She pulls another box closer to her. "I need to find it. That chain. You know, the chain of denim Luce made that year."

I certainly do know. Everybody in the family knows that story. So do a few people who aren't even related. Mama used to love to tell it. Even not being able to see her face, I can imagine that the story is running through her mind right now.

Luce absolutely hated the high school at first. Said his dad and I were sadistic to make him go there instead of another one he had applied and been accepted to. During the first weeks of his freshman year, he would remind us on a daily basis how archaic some of the rules were. Especially the one about no jeans allowed except on specified days. Well, one morning as Luce came out of his room ready to leave for school, I saw a lump under his shirt. I began to panic, thinking my son had developed a serious growth on his throat that I had somehow failed to notice. When he opened his shirt after I asked him to, I saw that he had hung swatches of denim on the gold chain he wore every day. Then he looked at me and said, "No one tells me what I can't wear."

Mama turns around and I'm sure I'm right about what she's thinking. I see the little smile. The one she always gets when she tells the very end of the story. How she said to Luce, "Bravo, son. That's the way to break a rule you feel is unfair, if you feel you must do so."

The smile goes away. Mama's eyes look like she's a little confused. Like she's been somewhere else and has had to return against her will. Eyes so sad I can hardly stand to look into them.

I stare down at my hands. At the little silver flowers Paula and I painted on each other's nails.

"Nail art, girlfriend. Don't you just love it!"

I wonder if I should hold out my hands to show her my nails. Say something about some of *my* drawings. The ones I *still* do. If this might get Mama's mind off the box of mostly Luce's drawings and bring her down from that ladder that's too short for her to be using in the first place to find things on the top shelf of the storage closet. And stop her eyes from looking like they do.

Dead.

But never wet.

Suddenly a picture crosses my mind of Mama right after

the services for Luce. How she looked when she had reached for the bright blue balloon being handed to her. Like she didn't know what was going on even though it was her idea that everybody there get a flower and a balloon as they were leaving.

The minister had explained it at the very end of the service. "Take a flower and keep it to help you remember the beautiful spirit that passed through our lives. Then let the balloon fly free in honor of that spirit."

For a minute it had looked like Mama couldn't figure out why she should have the balloon in her hand. She held on to it like she would never let it go. Even wrapped the string around her fingers two or three times.

Then she must have remembered what to do. She slowly opened her right hand and let the wind finally take the balloon. Dad had been standing on Mama's left side, holding her hand. I was on her other side. I had wanted to grab her right hand after it was empty and tell Mama I hadn't wanted to let go of my balloon either. But I didn't. The much too much sad eyes stopped me. Eyes so sad they couldn't even cry.

Mama starts climbing backward down the ladder. "Maybe Simon took that box to his office to look through it. I'll go see."

I've stood there, saying almost nothing the entire time. Now, feeling her squeeze past me to go down the hall to Dad's office, I wonder if Mama even realized I was there. Then I wonder something else. I wonder if I'm beginning to get an answer to a question I haven't realized was very important to ask.

Why am I obsessing about finding Luce's birth parents? Is there some sick part inside making me think that if I can show where Luce came from, Mama will stop missing him so much? That maybe then she'll remember how she gave birth to a child herself . . . ?

I'll probably never be able to talk to Mama about this—she probably doesn't want to hear it any more than I want to say it.

I wonder if I should talk to Aaron—
tell him everything

Would he think I was beyond strange?

We're going to the new park tomorrow and according to the weather report, it's going to be a spectacular day.

Maybe I should leave it at that—
just have a spectacular day without sharing any spectacular news

But I think I really want to tell him

❧ 28 ❧

I AGREE WITH AARON THAT THE NEW PARK IS spectacular, although I'm not as pumped up about it as he is. I *am* getting excited to tell him my news, but feel like I should wait until after he's seen more of the park.

Aaron talks about the park nonstop—the entire time we walk over the new bridge. It winds like a twisting silver ribbon across Lake Shore Drive. When we get to the highest point—which isn't all that high—he stops to take a picture of the new band shell pavilion.

"This design is awesome," he says, trying to get angles he wasn't able to get when we walked around and under the pavilion's ceiling of beams. I don't mention that laid out above the grass like it is, the pavilion reminds me of a lattice pie crust with silver curls at the end, arranged over a huge gob of green filling. It *is* cool, though.

On the way to the park Aaron had said we'd eat lunch there. I decide that will probably be the best time to tell him my news. I'm waiting patiently for that time to come, when suddenly we're right in front of the new fountain. I get almost as excited as Aaron has been. I am blown away!

Luce would have loved this!

This fountain is different from anything I have ever seen—or even imagined. Two tall, flat walls face each other over a straight stretch of concrete. The walls are about fifty feet high and made of glass blocks. Images of people's faces are projected onto the walls. Not famous stars, just regular people. They have different expressions on their faces—sometimes they're smiling and look happy, sometimes they look like they're in a state of wonder. Water pours over the top of each wall, making the huge faces shimmer. It splashes onto the concrete between the walls and turns that space into a shallow pool.

"Awesome!"

Aaron and I say the exact same thing at the same moment. Then before we can say another word, water spouts out of the pouting mouths of the twin faces. We both burst out laughing.

"This is really something!"

"Yep, it's fantastic. I could never have dreamed up something like this."

Aaron looks at me. "Oh, I don't know. I bet you can dream up some pretty amazing stuff."

"I do my share of dreaming up stuff, I guess. Like deciding to look through a phone book to start my search for my brother's biological parents."

I cannot *believe* it has flown out of my mouth just like that! While I'm standing there, getting splashed by the fantastic fountain, surrounded by all those people—all those screaming kids running under the pouring and spouting water to get drenched—I start blurting out my news.

I am *going nuts.*

"What did you say?"

I hope that Aaron's asking because he didn't hear me, but the expression on his face tells me that's not the reason.

"I said I looked in the telephone book to start my search for Luce's birth parents. It seemed like a reasonable place to start now that I know what their last name is. Or at least one of their last names."

Aaron catches my hand and pulls me back from the edge of the shallow pool. Away from where most of the people who have come to look at the fountain are standing. "Leah, are you serious?"

"I'm very serious. The name in the adoption decree is a pretty unusual last name, so I looked it up in the phone book. There're only eight listings with that name. And five of them live in the same area of the city."

I sound idiotic even to myself but I can't stop. I *have* to make Aaron understand.

"Okay. So it's not a sure thing. It's probably not even a good plan, but it's all I've got so far. I can't talk to my parents about it yet. I just can't. Not even to Dad, who would probably understand and might even help me. But I don't know if he would or not. And he probably doesn't know much anyway. I could tell from the decree and the lawyer's letter that it was a closed adoption. And, everything's got to start somewhere. . . ."

I'm running on and on like an imbecile. I can't seem to stop. Aaron holds my hand tighter and draws me farther away from the crowd and I keep explaining.

"I have to try, Aaron. I *have* to. Like I told you the other day—you know, while we were walking home after the Omnimax show—"

Aaron pulls me around to face him and puts the fingers of his free hand over my lips. I have to look into those clear, deep amber eyes. "Leah, Leah. Stop. I think I know how you feel. Really. And I admire the way you're so determined to go after what you want. I don't know if I completely agree with how you're going about it, but that's not my call. Even so, I'm good about all of it."

I feel tears behind my eyes and want to turn my head away but Aaron puts his fingers under my chin. "I care about you, Leah. So much."

Aaron's lips are soft and warm against my mouth. I don't try to pull away for even one second. Something I haven't imagined washes over me. Or maybe it's something I've just forgotten. It's a feeling of happiness. A brand-new happiness. All of it catches me so much by surprise I almost forget to breathe.

The smile in Aaron's eyes gives me courage to take my own chance. "I care for you, too, Aaron. Very much."

Aaron catches my other hand. "I *am* going to ask you to do one thing, though. Please, *please* think some more about talking to your parents. Okay?"

I nod my head.

I will. One day. Maybe even soon. But not until I'm completely ready and have done some more things totally on my own.

❧ 29 ❧

WHEN WE GET TO THE BUS STOP, PAULA TURNS AROUND and stands directly in front of me. Like putting herself between my body and the sign will keep me from leaving without her. "Are you sure, Leah? I don't mind—I mean, I'd really *like* to go with you."

It feels a little like Paula's trying too hard to sound sincere and I know why. A part of her is still trying to figure out why I want to get on the number 21 Cermak express bus, just like a part of me is. But the other part is that voice in my head that won't shut up. That other me.

Go on, girl, just do it. What do you have to lose?

We've come to Michigan Avenue so I can take the bus from there. After I leave, Paula will go to the library to wait until I get back. Her mother thinks that's where we'll both be. Mama thinks the same thing. I told her we were going to the library to look through some college catalogs. I knew she'd have no objections to that.

It seemed like she didn't care where I was going.

"Leah?" Paula's big eyes look worried.

I smile. "I'm sure, Paula. Really. And I know you'd go if I asked you, but I kind of want to do this by myself . . . you know."

"Yeah, I know." Paula's smile is trying hard to be real.

I look down the street again. When I turn back, I see a big question on Paula's face. "What?"

"Ah . . . well, Leah, I'm just wondering what you're going to do when you get there. You know, to the . . . ah, the neighborhood."

I've been wondering that myself.

I shrug my shoulders. "I'll figure it out when I get there." I turn back to look down the street again.

Come on, bus. Please. Get here before I lose my nerve.

Paula keeps standing there. All of it is beginning to make me nervous. "Paula, please go on to the library. I'll be fine. Honest."

"I know you'll be okay. I just thought . . . I just want to wait with you." She grins. "Maybe I just want to make sure you get on that bus. You know, that you're not sneaking off somewhere."

"Darn. You guessed it." I pretend to look guilty. "I'm getting on the bus to keep a secret rendezvous with the very mysterious Wonder Who!"

This time Paula's laugh is real. "Yeah. Right. Like you'd even *think* of having a rendezvous with anybody besides Aaron James the magnificent. And there's no way you'd keep that a secret from me, girlfriend, *especially* since it was me who hooked you two up in the first place."

"Don't worry, I'll never forget that." I wink at Paula. "I'll make sure you're first on the list of people invited to the elopement."

Paula and I are still laughing when number 21 Cermak express rolls to a stop.

The bus isn't crowded. I get a window seat right at the front and have a good view of everything we pass.

At first it's easy to keep track of where I am. After a few blocks we pass the Italian restaurant with the red-and-gold scalloped awning. Dad's favorite.

"One of the best Italian kitchens in Chicago!"

Yeah, Dad. Like you've been in most of them.

The bus stays on the same street, passing a string of places. Businesses. Markets, beauty shops, pharmacies, coffee shops, currency exchanges, day-care centers . . . It's like one string with attachments that goes on for a few blocks and then ends so a new one can unroll. The names and colors of the attachments are different but the string is still the same. More markets, beauty shops, pharmacies, coffee shops, currency exchanges, day-care centers . . .

After about twenty or so blocks, I've seen enough to be pretty sure I've never been in this part of the city before. Since all the places are beginning to look alike, I start noticing the people on the street.

What am I looking for?

I know from the CTA route map I printed out from the Internet that I should stay on this bus until it makes its first turn onto another street. Even so I pay close attention to each street name we pass. I'm so busy keeping track of signs that a long building with a familiar pattern across the top of it doesn't register until we're almost in front of it.

The Mexican Fine Arts Center Museum!

It's the museum Paula and I wrote about for our art team project last year. We went there at least four times to see exhibits, make sketches, and interview docents. I never paid attention to the exact location since somebody always drove us.

Luce brought us once when he was home on spring break.

I lean over to the driver. "Excuse me, how soon will you be turning off Eighteenth?"

"After the next two blocks."

I get up to stand by the door so I can get off when the bus stops at the corner coming up. It's more than four blocks away from where I was headed, but it's the right place to be.

Seeing this museum is a sign. I just know it is!

❧ 30 ❧

I TURN THE CORNER TO HEAD DOWN THE SIDEWALK that passes the front entrance of the museum. There aren't many people on the street, probably because it's early in the afternoon. I'm directly in front of the museum in what seems like seconds.

Being around something familiar makes me start to relax a little. I'm even tempted to go inside the museum and look around to see what new exhibits are there. To say hi to Mr. Ortiz who was so nice about helping Paula and me with our report.

Get real. You're not on a sightseeing tour.

I make myself keep walking.

Down the street on the other side of the museum is a small park. I stop by the chain-link fence and look around. There're only a few kids out playing. Baby-swing ages. A couple of women are sitting on a bench, watching the kids and talking. At the other end of the fenced-in area a small group of old men are standing, pitching horseshoes. Nobody pays any attention to me. I keep on toward the end of the street.

It's amazing how being just one block from the main street changes everything. There's no string of businesses. No office buildings. There're a few small apartment buildings, but mostly there are just houses. Small, neat one- and two-story houses. Most of them close to the street with porches on the same level as the sidewalk.

A regular street where anybody might live.

A boy on a scooter is headed down the sidewalk. His head is packed with dark curls.

Like Luce's used to be when he was little.

I move close to the edge of the sidewalk so he can get by. He smiles when he passes. I smile back and decide to turn down the street behind him.

It gets quieter as I keep walking down the street. There's no traffic, no people. The sounds of the kids in the park are far away. The soft *click-click*s of the scooter wheels crossing sidewalk cracks begin to fade. A screen door slams shut when a woman who was sitting on her porch with a baby gets up to go into her house. Now I see no other person on the street but me.

I try to notice everything without staring. The small trees

squeezed between the houses. The fancy iron bars across many of the windows and doors. And the flowers that are everywhere they can possibly be. Growing out of big pots and window boxes and from every inch of dirt in the narrow yards that hasn't been covered over with cement.

When I stop at the end of the second block and try to figure out whether or not to cross over to the other side, Paula's question runs through my mind.

What are you going to do when you get there?

I start to wonder why I hadn't at least thought up a reason to go up to the houses and knock on the doors. To have a reason to see the people who live in these houses. To talk to them.

What was I thinking? Did I imagine there was going to be a people parade in the neighborhood?

I try to come up with a reason.

"Hi. I'm taking a survey for a school project. . . ."

No good. School's out. Summer school probably doesn't give projects. And I'm not carrying anything to write on like I would be if I were out to take a survey.

"Excuse me. I'm lost. Could I use your phone . . . ?"

Who would I call or even pretend to be calling? What would I say?

❀ ❀ ❀

You're an idiot, Leah. You weren't thinking at all!

The only thing I can think of is to keep walking. At least down this block and maybe the next. Maybe some other people would be sitting on their porches. Maybe I would get really lucky and . . .

And what?

I look down the street ahead. Blocks that look pretty much like this one. More neat little houses with narrow yards for their flowers and small trees squeezed in between.

Leah, you are definitely *an idiot!*

I stop where I am—right in the middle of the block.

What on earth are you thinking? What could you possibly be looking for? What do you want to find?

For the first time I know I *have* to answer the questions. At least tell *myself* the truth.

Aaron's voice goes through my head. What he said after we left the fountain to walk through the rest of Millennium Park. "Leah, is there something you need to find out about Luce—like, maybe, something you think *he* might have wanted to know about himself?"

Luce was perfectly happy with himself. Every kid should be as satisfied with himself as he was.

"Or is there something *you* need to know about him that you don't already know? Something really important?"

I hadn't given Aaron any answers to his questions. I just kept walking beside him, holding his hand. Keeping my eyes on the ground so I wouldn't trip over the crisscrossing paths that run through the park in all directions.

Now, standing alone on the sidewalk in the middle of a block in a neighborhood I've never even seen before, much less been in, my answer spits out.

"I WANT TO FIND ANOTHER LUCE!"

My hand automatically flies up to cover my mouth. But it's too late. The words are already out. I heard them even though I can hardly believe I've said them. And so loud! For nobody and *any*body to hear.

I stand there like I'm frozen, staring at the house that I'm in front of. It's painted a pretty deep blue.

Luce's favorite color.

For an instant I imagine that if I were inside that sweet little house, I would see an almost-tall, slender man. Or man-becoming, as Dad would say. Somebody who usually leaves his socks wherever they land when he takes them off. A face with a skinny new mustache that always smiles back at its own image in the mirror first thing in the morning.

"Bibi says a smile ought to begin everybody's day. I give one to myself to make sure!"

"Oh Luce. If only I could find you again!"

What's delivered to my head straight from my heart has come out again. Only this time it feels like I've said it out loud on purpose. And just for me.

I look again at the pretty blue house. Somebody might be inside watching, ready to call the police to tell them to come and get the crazy girl who's out on the street talking to herself. I turn around and head back the way I came. Back to the museum. The one place in this neighborhood that makes *any* sense for me to be.

I stop on the first landing of the entrance and catch my breath. Then I look behind me at the rows of houses that go on for blocks. Most with pots or boxes of flowers. Probably some with people whose last names are the same as the one on the letter and document I found in Dad's junky drawer.

For the third time that day something from deep inside me comes out. Only this time it's not words. More like a sigh. I hear it while I stand there under that ancient design of the Zapotec people. It turns into a pain as I watch visitors make their way inside the museum to see treasures of beautiful civilizations that are lost forever.

I wonder if it's really like Mrs. Robinson said when we were
reading The Tale of Two Cities
that it's always the best of times and the worst of times, like
Dickens said in the first line

and not only when revolutions are going on

best and worst times can be together
at the same time,
anytime
like now for me

except I would say
it's the worst of times and almost the best of times

I don't think anything can ever be the best again,
but I do think it can get better.

❧ 31 ❦

IT'S THE BEST PART OF THE DAY WHEN BIBI AND I START our morning walk. The sun is bright and air is still cool, especially by the lake. A perfect time.

I notice that Bibi's walking a lot slower than usual. "Maybe we shouldn't be taking this route to your garden, Bibi. Let's cut over now and go through the museum yard."

"*My* garden? I would think by now it was *our* garden." Bibi links her arm through mine. "No, baby. And in case you're wondering, I'm not languishing. Just enjoying this lovely August day."

Neither of us talks much as we keep down the lake path. We hardly ever do when we walk here. I think we both like silence while we watch the water.

Except when I'm with Aaron.

Thinking about Aaron makes it hard to keep from smiling. How much fun we've had these last few weeks. The bicycle rides along the lake just before dark. Our fast-food-nics—what we named times we pick up something from a fast-food place and sit somewhere outside to eat.

We even had fun at his family reunion, which both of us had been a little nervous about going to. Aaron laughed out loud at the big banquet table when I whispered how I had counted thirteen of his relatives with amber eyes.

Being with Aaron keeps me from going crazy while I try to figure out once and for all the answer to my big question, the one he likes to put in the words of Shakespeare: "To find or not to find Luce's birth parents: *that* is the question."

I grin whenever I remember the day he dreamed that up.

It was our first library date—and that kind of date mostly because it was rainy and almost cold outside.

"I like to walk in the rain," I lied to Aaron when he suggested going to the library. "It can be quite invigorating."

"Yeah, right." Aaron kept pulling me down the street toward the big iron double doors of the huge building that takes up most of the block. "Well, I *don't* like walking in the rain. To me it's just plain soggy."

We spent most of that afternoon in the library—the Harold Washington Library Center. It's pretty cool. Especially the Winter Garden on the ninth floor. The space is over a hundred feet high, stretching to a skylight. I enjoyed just standing there, watching the rain fall above us.

But Aaron thought it would be more "enjoyable" to go to the seventh floor and look through what he said was "some of the greatest poetry ever written." Yep, good old Shakespeare.

And that's what we did for what seemed like hours. We looked through musty books of old, *old* poetry. For me the most enjoyable part was Aaron telling me about Hamlet, this prince who thinks about killing himself after he finds out that his new stepfather, who was also his uncle before he married his mother, had killed his father. Everything is so messed up, but it actually does make a really great play.

He picked out parts of it for us to read together. Sections that the famous soliloquies are in. That's when Aaron said that in a way Hamlet's soliloquy "To be or not to be: that is the question" made him think of my big question.

"Not that you're trying to decide between salvation or redemption, like Hamlet was. But what you decide about Luce's birth parents *can* affect the rest of your life."

Yeah, it could. Maybe.

I'm so busy remembering, I don't realize Bibi and I have gone beyond the best underpass for getting to the garden. The next one is all the way on the other side of the Museum of Science and Industry, which is now between where we are on the lake path and the garden. I look at my grandmother. "Bibi, are you sure you still—"

"Leah, stop acting like I'm an old lady. Yes, I'm sure I still want to go to *our* garden." Bibi starts walking faster, tugging at my arm to make me keep up with her. She keeps up that pace until we get there.

Over the summer she and I have come to the garden about once a week. She's almost convinced me that a garden *can* be interesting. Almost. But it has been amazing to see the changes that happen from week to week. Sometimes from day to day—especially during the hot spell in July when the bellflowers seemed to spring open overnight.

"Which way should we head first? Want to check out the lobelia or see how the golden showers are doing?" I grin at Bibi, knowing I'm blowing her away with my fabulous perennial knowledge.

The look on her face is almost as good as the hug she gives me. "Leah, you thrill my heart."

We start making our way around the middle circle that lets us see things in every direction. I don't know whether it's the beautiful flowers that are everywhere, the sunshine-bright day, the thoughts about Aaron, or what. But all of a sudden I know that I *have* to tell Bibi some of the things that have been on my mind.

"Bibi, there's something else I've been trying to learn

about this summer." I take a big breath. "I've been trying to find out something about Luce's birth parents."

Once I start, it's easy to tell her everything. We keep moving around the circle while I talk, and for most of the time she keeps her eyes on the grass while she listens, walking slower and slower. When I get the part about being on the street by the museum, she stops altogether. But she doesn't look up at me until I finish.

For a long time after I'm not saying anything else, she doesn't say a word. I worry that maybe I've upset her.

"Bibi, I don't mean to—"

She looks at me and shakes her head. Then she takes my hand and pulls me to the stone steps leading up from the lower inner circle to the circles above. Bursts of lavender-blue pincushions are on either side of us.

"Have you talked to your parents about this?" Before I can answer, Bibi shakes her head again. "Of course you haven't. I'm not thinking. You would have said so if you had."

She rests one of her feet on the steps that are too low for us to sit on. "Why did you decide *not* to talk to them about this?"

It's my turn to look down. I shrug. "I just haven't."

Tiny white butterflies move among the flowers. I remember

Bibi telling me how pincushions are one of the perennials that attract butterflies. That's one of the reasons I like them. That plus the fact that close up, each bloom looks like a cushion with teeny-tiny straight pins in it.

"I don't think it's time to talk to them about it, I guess."

Bibi links her arm through mine so that I'll start walking again with her. For a while she doesn't say anything while she heads to the edge of the outer upper circle. When we get there, she stops and looks into my face.

"You know, Leah, one of the things I keep learning as I grow older is that sometimes it's extra hard to keep on with the business of living. Now, listening to you, I'm beginning to think—no, make that beginning to *know*. Yes. Leah, I *know* that you're doing that better than any of the rest of us in the family."

I don't know what to say and want to look away, but I don't.

"In one way it doesn't really matter what you decide to do. What does matter is that you're crossing over some difficult ground. Taking steps to put things in perspective."

Bibi's arm tightens against mine. "None of us can ever put Luce's death behind us. We will never even want to. But we all have to move on."

I start hearing the city sounds. And, although they're

always visible over the trees around the edges of our garden park, I notice the churchlike windows of the Jackson Towers apartments.

Bibi moves closer. "And I think you're ready to help someone else we both love very much take a few hard steps over that ground. Your mother. My dear, grieving daughter. Alexis."

This time I can't stop myself from looking away from my grandmother's face. "There's nothing I can do, Bibi. I can't help Mama. She doesn't want my help. She never . . . she won't let me."

I wish I could tell Bibi the whys but I know I shouldn't. That I can't even as they march across my brain.

Mama doesn't care what I think, Bibi. Or do, for that matter. Does she pay any *attention to me? She hasn't said one thing about how much I go out with Aaron. Does she even* know *how much? She didn't even notice that I cut my bangs. At least not until Dad said how nice they looked. Then she* had *to say something since we were all sitting there at breakfast.*

Bibi puts her finger under my chin to lift my head. To get me to look at her. It's like Aaron did that first time in the park. The memory of it forces me to almost smile, even though most of what I feel inside has started to make me want to cry.

"You *can*, sweetheart. You can do *everything* for Lexie that she needs right now." Bibi smiles at me and then winks. "Why, you found out some things about perennials even *I* didn't know. That's a sure sign you can do anything!"

I don't say anything and Bibi doesn't say any more. In the quiet that stays between us while we walk home through the noisy rush-hour world, one thought keeps running through my mind.

I wonder if Mama cares about me at all?

❧ 32 ❧

IT DOESN'T HAPPEN LIKE I PLANNED. NOT EVEN CLOSE!

I thought about what Bibi said for almost a week. A week of watching Mama and thinking that maybe Bibi was right. Then watching her some more and deciding Bibi wasn't even *close* to right. And back to "okay, I will," and then back again to "no way."

It's bizarre, but it was Mama's eyes that made me finally decide something. One night after dinner she was sitting in the kitchen talking on the phone to her friend in Maryland. Whatever she was listening to cracked her up. She started laughing so hard I turned around from the sink where I was washing dishes to look at her. And I saw her eyes.

They weren't even close to laughing. They weren't even smiling. They were just the same sad eyes.

Bibi's right about one thing—somebody's *got to do something for Mama. I guess there'll be no harm in me trying.*

I decided to invite Mama to lunch with me. I would use

some of my baby-sitting and dog-walking money to treat. That would catch her by surprise. Then, while we were at lunch, we would talk.

It was an excellent plan. Especially deciding to write Mama an invitation instead of just asking her face to face. In the invitation I put the names of three neighborhood restaurants and asked her to circle the one she'd like to go to. I also listed three dates and times and asked her to check the one she wanted.

I decided to slip the invitation into her purse. She usually hangs the one she's using on her bedroom door. I didn't plan on looking through the purse, just to slip in my invitation and maybe leave the purse open a little to make it easy for her to spot. But when I opened her purse, a pile of stuff stacked near the top started falling out.

All of it was photographs. Snapshots. I was able to grab some to keep them from falling on the floor. When I picked up those that had, I automatically started looking at them.

The pictures were of Luce. His third-grade picture. His fourth- and fifth-grade pictures. Luce with his hair slicked back with grease when he entered the seventh-grade break-dancing competition.

Mama couldn't stand the way he looked that night!

There were the before and after pictures. The ones Dad

put together on the computer to show Luce before he had braces and after the braces were off. Luce dressed in tails the time he was the ring bearer at Cousin Karen's wedding.

I started flipping through the pictures. Baby pictures. Luce laughing like crazy while he's pulling down his diaper. Then standing in the hall without a stitch on and a big paper bag over his head.

Graduation pictures. Luce at his eighth-grade graduation, wearing his new suit and tennis shoes. Luce standing between Bibi and Grandma Myrtle after the ceremonies, all of them laughing.

I flipped through them faster and faster.

They're all of Luce. Every single one.

The last picture was one from the scrapbook Luce and I made Dad for his fiftieth birthday. All of the pictures are of Dad and the two of us. In this one Dad's lying on his back, asleep, with baby Luce lying on Dad's chest, also asleep.

At least there's one of Dad, but there's none of me. None!

I had just decided that this definitely *wouldn't* be a good time to sneak an invitation into Mama's purse when I heard her coming down the hall. I rushed to put the stack of pictures back into her purse, forgetting about the note that was also in my hand. It went into the purse with everything else, sandwiched between a couple of the photos.

When Mama handed the note back to me the next day without saying anything, I thought she was probably irritated that I had been in her purse. That just handing me the note was her way of letting me know *she* knew I had invaded her privacy. But when I looked at her, she seemed to be almost smiling.

I looked at the note. She had made her choices, drawing a little face with a surprised expression beside each—Café Bono for lunch, Saturday afternoon.

Now it's Friday evening. Mama and I are shopping for groceries. Since Dad does most of the cooking, she usually does most of the shopping. I'm not sure why I said I'd go with her when she asked except that I thought it might help me get up the rest of my nerve for having the talk I planned to have in the first place, even after changing my mind about wanting to have it, but finally decided that we might as well go on and have anyway.

Geez! You can't even think *straight.*

I push the grocery cart, following behind Mama who's paying close attention to the detailed list Dad always gives her for each item we're supposed to get. Dad's extra-picky about everything his recipes call for.

I've decided that the best thing to do when Mama and

I are at lunch tomorrow is to get right to the point.

I'll bring it up right after the waiter has taken our orders.

I push along behind Mama, practicing what I'm going to say tomorrow. Trying to choose the best words and arrangements the same way she's shopping for ingredients.

Mama, did you ever think about not *telling Luce he was adopted? Do you ever wish you hadn't?*

Mama examines every single carrot in a fresh bunch before tossing the whole thing into the basket.

Did you and Luce ever talk about his birth parents?

Mama asks me to pick out some red potatoes. "About eight. Make sure they're a nice size."

Mama, how would you have felt if Luce started tracking down his birth parents?

Mama looks at the potatoes I've picked out and dropped in a plastic bag. "Good. Now, how about selecting three or four nice garlic bulbs."

Did you worry that maybe if he found his biological family, he might want to be with them?

I have trouble keeping my mind on picking out the garlic. I'm not sure what makes one bulb of garlic nicer than another.

Do you think a person automatically loves his biological family more—you know, because everybody's related by blood?

Mama has trouble finding the type of pasta Dad put on the list and asks me to look across the stacks of pasta packages, too. I start running my fingers along the edge of the top shelf to keep my mind on what we're looking for.

Do you think parents love their children equally the same no matter whether they're biological or not?

"There it is, Leah. Right there above your fingers. See? Penne pasta. It's that box sticking out a little."

When I lift my hand to pull out the box of pasta, I accidentally knock over the one next to it. Then that box pushes into the ones next to and behind it. In only seconds rows of pasta boxes and bags tumble into each other like dominoes, with half of them crashing down to the floor. Some of them break open. Curl-, stick-, twist-, and pea-shaped pieces spill across the floor. It's like a crazy collection of kindergarten art supplies.

Mama and I both stand there, looking at the mess that has spread down half the aisle. I know she's wondering how it all happened, just like I am. I open my mouth to explain that the boxes must have been only half stacked. That whoever stacked them must have been stupid. Or lazy. Or both. That the person was probably a worthless idiot. That's what I'm ready to say when I hear the most amazing words.

They shoot out of my mouth loud and clear like some

other words did that day in the neat little neighborhood. Words that must have been pushed around, on top of, and in between stuff buried so deep inside me that I'm almost surprised to know they're there.

"Mama, did you love Luce more than me because he was your first child? Did you even *want* any more children after you got Luce?"

I hear the words and wonder if I've gone completely crazy.

❧ 33 ❧

I HAVE TROUBLE KEEPING TRACK OF WHAT HAPPENED next and then after that. Did Mama say, "Who *cares* about that mess on the floor" before the manager said, "I'm sorry, Mrs. Clair," or after? Did the stock boy carrying the long bushy broom slip and fall on the mess before I started laughing-crying or after? Did we pay for the groceries Mama left by the number six checkout counter and leave them there for delivery or just walk off without doing anything? Is that why the girl with the big Eloise button on her shirt kept staring at us?

Mama's hand holding mine while we head to our car is just tight enough so I don't want to let go. "Mama, I'm sorry. I—"

"*Sh, shhhhhhhh.*" Mama leans over so her head touches the side of mine. I smell her green tea scent. It's from the bath oil she pours in the tub by the gallon, making that whole part of our apartment smell like spring. "Don't you be sorry about anything, Leah. Not one single thing."

When we get to the car, Mama beeps open the locked doors and walks with me to the passenger side. She opens the door, but before I can get in she puts her arms around me and pulls me close to her. Then closer.

Ahhhh . . . I had almost forgotten what this feels like.

We stand like that right there beside our car in the parking lot of the supermarket and I don't care even a little if anybody's watching and thinks we're strange.

We're still parked in the lot while Mama and I sit in the car, not saying anything. I'm still crying. Then I wonder if Mama's crying a little, too. She's not making noise like I am, but it seems like she's reaching for more tissues than she's handing to me.

After a while I feel like I can start to say something. I take a getting-ready breath, but then Mama holds up her hand to stop me.

"Leah, please just let me say something first. I need to get this out. I promise that after I do, I'll listen without a peep to anything—*every*thing—you want to say. Promise. Not one peep!"

Mama looks at me. I nod my head. She takes her getting-ready breath.

"I never told this to you or to . . . to Luce." It's hard for Mama to say his name out loud, just like it has been for me. "The fact of it is, I never thought about having children. It wasn't that I *didn't* want any; I just wasn't sure that I *did*. The only thing I was absolutely sure about was that I wanted to be married to Simon Clair. "

Mama looks out the window. A man passing by looks at her and smiles. She turns back to me.

"Simon . . . your father wanted children very much. Probably as much as he wanted me." Mama laughs. It's more to herself than me. "Some of that probably comes from being from such a large, loving family."

I don't push the picture of Dad's family out of my head. Grandma Myrtle with all of the children she says she'd rather have had than all the money in the world. Dad standing next to Aunt Monique. My favorite of all of them.

"We never really discussed it seriously, but I was careful not to get pregnant. I think your father thought I couldn't and I did nothing to correct that thought."

Mama looks down at the seat and picks at something. "Yes, I'm sure I gave him that impression."

She's embarrassed.

I look down at my jeans and wait for her to go on.

"After three years and without saying anything to me,

Simon went to an agency to get information. Ask questions."

Rock-A-Bye.

I stay quiet.

"After his second visit he told me what had been on his mind. Almost like an obsession, he said. How he had gone to this agency, talked to one of the counselors."

Maybe getting obsessed is in my genes.

Mama looks down at the scratch on the seat she's been picking at. "He even told me about all the pictures of families he saw—families with children. . . ."

And babies, Mama. Lots of babies.

I drop my eyes and hope Mama doesn't notice my smile.

"What I heard most as I listened to Simon was how *much* he wanted a child. And as soon as possible. But in my heart I still wasn't convinced, certainly not to the point of deciding to try to get pregnant."

Mama turns away from me to look out the car window again. For a few seconds she's quiet. I am, too. She's still looking in that direction when she starts talking again. "But that same heart knew it had to make Simon happy any way I could. So on the third and rest of the visits I was at the agency with him."

When Mama turns back so I can see her face, tears are beginning to pour down her cheeks. She doesn't lift her hands to wipe them away. "I think I loved Luce from the first moment I held him. That's what my heart remembers. But, of course, it would have been impossible not to. Even as a baby, he was as sweet as he was beautiful."

Her tears fall harder. Almost in splashes. I want to reach out to Mama but think that if I do she might stop talking, so I don't.

"And after only a little while I began to realize that this bright, beautiful, and loving child was giving *me* an extraordinary gift. Because of him, I was learning a lesson I thought I had already mastered: I was learning truly *how* to love."

My tears start falling as fast and hard as Mama's. I don't wipe mine away either.

"Having those chubby sweet-smelling arms . . . seeing them reach out for me . . ." Mama sounds like she's choking. I still don't know what I should do. I'm relieved when she keeps talking.

"Seeing the trust in the eyes above those arms, well, that's one of the things that made me truly ready to fill my home with children. Ready *and* anxious to have you!"

Mama reaches over to pull me into her arms. When I get close to her, both of us are crying so hard I can hardly tell which wet face belongs to whom. She keeps talking while she holds me. "And when they put this sweet baby girl into my waiting arms on January twenty-second, more happiness than I knew existed on this earth rushed into my heart to live forever."

We stay like that for a long time. Mama and me. It's almost like we're wrapped together in this soft cocoon. Only better.

I lift up my head. Mama keeps her arm around me as she sits back and puts her hands on the steering wheel. Like she's supporting herself and me. For a long minute she doesn't say anything. Then she turns again and looks at me.

"You know, when it first happened . . . when Luce . . . when he died, I couldn't stop blaming myself."

You didn't have anything to do with it, Mama. You weren't even in that stupid car. And you were always *telling Luce not to hot-rod.*

A mixed-up combination of awful feelings rushes through me. Like sharp knives hurling themselves through me from different directions. The feelings make me almost laugh at Mama's "hot-rod" expression that Luce and I always made fun of.

"You sound like your own grandmother, Ma."

The feelings make me almost start crying hard all over again when I hear how awfully, horribly sad Mama sounds.

But what I feel most is mad. *Furious* mad!

Luce, LUCE! Do you see what you did? Do you have any idea how you made everything?

I want to punch my fist right through the windshield. I almost do when the awful thought slams into my head.

Luce's head crashed into the windshield. . . .

I can feel my body twitching. I know I'm absolutely not going to be able to stand it. Then I hear something coming from far away. Mama's voice, a lot softer than before.

"When Simon and I . . . after we got the news, I don't remember how long after, I went into the drawer where we keep the scrapbooks. You know. . . ."

The built-in drawers in the storage closet. The top one. Yeah, I know.

"I stood right there in that dark closet and took out picture after picture. Of Luce. Pictures . . . Luce frozen in time. The Luce that could never be taken away from me."

Mama's voice starts breaking up. I push myself closer to her without even realizing I'm moving. She keeps talking in the wavery voice.

"The minute I started holding those pictures, putting them in my purse so I could have them with me wherever I went, I started asking myself over and over if I loved him enough."

The breaking up in her voice gets worse. "Maybe I didn't.

Maybe I didn't love him enough in the beginning. The way I loved you even as you slept under my heart. Maybe I didn't pull him in close enough, hold on to him tight enough. The way I've always tried to do with you. Maybe that's why I lost him."

I'm so close to Mama by now I'm almost on top of her. "But Mama, that can't be true. We *all* loved Luce so much. You and Dad and Bibi and me. Everybody! And we *all* lost him."

The words come out automatically just like the next thing I do when Mama starts to cry again. No, not just crying. She starts *bawling* like a tiny little baby.

I put my arms around her. I hold her as tight and as close as I can. After a few seconds it begins to feel like I'm also wrapping my arms around myself.

❧ 34 ❧

"AND WHAT ABOUT YOU, MRS. CLAIR? YOU READY TO try that grilled portabella sandwich or are you going to settle on the usual? You know, a cheeseburger?"

Mama wrinkles her nose when she smiles at our waitress. Marcy. We always try to sit at one of her tables when we come to Café Bono. "Young lady, I recall vividly coming here with my son and thinking you and he were in a conspiracy about my ordering habits. So I'm going to give you a treat." She slams her menu shut. "In honor of my son the vegetarian *and* in celebration of my daughter who's treating today, I'm going to have the portabella mushroom and cheese sandwich, but hold the grilled onions and double the tomato. Instead of fries, I'll have the fruit salad. Okay?"

"All right!" Marcy gives Mama the thumbs-up sign and a big grin. "Luce would be proud! Anything to drink?"

"Just water, thanks."

It's a little strange hearing Mama and Marcy. Both of

them talking about Luce like that. But at the same time it doesn't *feel* strange at all. Luce *would* have been happy to see Mama order a vegetarian sandwich. He was always on her case about how much meat she eats.

"Your body's got to work real hard to digest all that meat, Ma. Remember, that body ain't as young as it used to be, you know."

"Listen, young man, you just keep tabs on your *body. I'll take care of mine."*

When I look across the table at Mama, I can almost hear the Luce and Mama duet. The together high-low laughter.

I've been thinking all morning about the best way to get our conversation started. After yesterday I'm pretty sure it's going to be okay to talk to Mama, but I'm still not certain how to bring it up.

Just say it.

I smile, hearing that other me talking, telling me as usual what to do. Mama looks at me and smiles back. "What?"

"Ah, nothing." I want to take the words back as soon as they're out. "I mean, ah, it's something. I mean, it's nothing that I'm smiling at, but there *is* something. . . ."

I make myself stop.

Get it together.

"Mama, I—"

Mama holds up her hand the way she did in the car when she wanted me to stop. I do.

"I don't want to cut you off, but there's something I want to confess before you go on. Okay?"

"Okay." I sit back in my chair.

"Last night after you had gone to your room, your father, Bibi, and I had a little talk."

There must be a reaction on my face because Mama interrupts what she was about to say. "It wasn't about you, baby, although it ended up with us wondering what we could do to help you."

Help me?

Mama must have read my face again. "Look, I'm saying this badly. Let me start again. While we were talking, Bibi told us about . . . she explained how you were interested in learning about . . . well, finding out about Luce's birth parents."

Bibi told?

It's like it's my *face* and Mama who are having the conversation. She answers what she sees in it again. "Wait a minute, baby. Please don't think your grandmother betrayed a confidence. She didn't. She wouldn't. She said something about it because of something *I* said. She thought you had already mentioned it to me—about tracking Luce's biological roots. She said you and she had talked about it about a week ago and that she had encouraged you to talk to me. She thought you had and that I already knew."

I hadn't really thought Bibi would betray me. I don't think she ever would. But I'm wondering what all of them were talking about for the subject of my finding Luce's birth parents to come up.

Mama reaches over the table and takes my hand. I look in her face and think she's seen again what I'm wondering about.

"Leah, last night your father and I were wondering out loud with Bibi how on earth we might even begin helping you as much as you've helped us these past few months.

Helped you? I've helped you and *Dad?*

This time I don't even wonder if my face has shown what I want to say. I just wait for Mama to go on.

"Oh yes, baby. You've helped us. So much more than you will ever know. So much more than I hope I will ever have to tell you."

Mama rubs my hand, pats it, and then pulls hers back. "But let me tell you about that later, okay? I definitely don't want to get the waterworks started again right now. I want to be ready to enjoy every bite of this portabella and cheese sandwich."

Then it's like this lunch is being conducted by somebody

standing over us. Like a puppeteer is controlling everything in the restaurant, pulling strings at just the right moment to get us to say certain things, make other things happen. Right after Mama said that, Marcy appears with our orders.

"Enjoy, folks. I'll be back in a sec to make sure everything's okay!"

"Thanks, Marcy." I start examining my tuna burger to make sure they didn't include any tomatoes on it while they were doubling them on Mama's sandwich.

"Okay. I guess I'd better get going with this new experience."

I look over at Mama. I want to see if what I heard in her voice is on her face. It is. I can't keep from giggling.

"Yuk. My son had excellent taste in many things, but not in sandwiches."

Mama and I laugh together.

Our very own special duet.

❧ 35 ❧

"SHE SAID SHE'D HELP YOU?"

"Yep. Whenever I was ready. Even before I'm eighteen, if that's what I want."

"What's being eighteen got to do with it?"

"It's like this. As a relative of the adopted person, I can start a search on my own when I'm twenty-one. With my parents' consent I can start when I'm eighteen."

Paula's big eyes look at me over the burger she's biting into. What she picked up for the fast-foodnic she and I are having. Her eyes are almost as wide and round as the bun.

"Mama said if I wanted to do the search right away, she'd be the point person. You know, the one to be contacted."

Paula finishes chewing the pile of fries she stuffed into her mouth. "Leah, do you think way deep down your mom wants to find out like you do?"

I look out over the lake, hearing Mama's voice in my head.

"I'll never be able to think of Luce as anything but my son.

Simon's and mine. Your brother. In my mind and heart he will always belong just to us. But I can honestly understand it if that's not enough for you. And I'll help you in any way I can."

I twirl the bottle top Paula put down on the picnic table. "I really don't think so. But I'm sure she'll help me if that's what I want to do."

"So?"

"'So' what?"

"So you know what I mean, girl. Don't be obtuse."

"Listen to you—Miss Fancy Talk!"

"Leah . . ."

I have to laugh. "Okay, okay."

I look down the bike path our picnic table is near. It winds up a little hill and then disappears into a small group of trees. For about the hundredth time, something else Mama told me yesterday sits in my mind.

"If only I had had a tiny warning . . . any hint of the possibility that the last time just the two of us talked would be . . . I think I was a little cross with him when he called home earlier that day. . . . I fussed at him about talking on his cell phone while he was driving. . . . Sometimes I believe that the only thing I really, really want to do when it comes to Luce is to make myself believe without any doubt that he knew how so very much I loved him. . . ."

While she was talking in the restaurant, waterworks got started with both of us, but neither of us had cared. Now it seems like they're about to get started again.

Enough, Leah. Enough!

I look at Paula. "I haven't decided. I really haven't." I reach over and put my hand on hers. "Don't think I'm crazy, but . . ." I wonder if I should go on.

"But what? Tell me, Leah." She laces her fingers through mine. "You know I would never call you crazy. At least not to your face."

I squeeze her fingers while we laugh. "Sometimes . . . well, I think it might be nice just to imagine that somewhere out there in the world there just might be a person related by blood to Luce . . . you know, somebody who's like him."

Paula doesn't smile or snicker. I keep on. "You know, somebody with curly hair that sticks out a little at the top, with those same brown eyes that almost disappear into his face when he gets really tickled. And underneath every beautiful thing you see on the outside of that person, there'd be a good heart and a wonderful spirit."

I throw out a crust left from my sandwich to gulls pecking around near us. "If I search for Luce's birth relatives, maybe I'd find out for sure that there wasn't any chance for this person to exist. But if I don't search, I wouldn't know for sure and I might keep on imagining and . . ."

I stop myself. Even to me I'm sounding a little nuts.

"You could keep on hoping." Paula taps my nose with her finger as she smiles at me. "And that might be a good thing, too."

"Yeah."

"So what do you think you're going to do?"

"The only thing I can do. Figure out what I want to do."

Both of us throw the rest of our leftover food to the gulls, looking out at the lake and listening to their cooing-pecking sounds. The only ones around.

Dear Luce,

Somewhere in the deepest part of myself (you know—the part Bibi calls the most honest place), I have to believe that you know what I've been up to. I hope it hasn't made you mad. If it has I hope you'll forgive me, or if you can't, that you'll keep loving me. I don't think I can ever forgive you for dying, but I will always, **ALWAYS** love you. More than I ever got a chance to tell you in person.

I don't know if I'll find what I'm looking for or even if I'll keep looking. Mahri says I'm already more curious than driven and that curiosity fades, so we'll see.

I've gotten to love Mahri, Luce. She misses you so so so much like we all do, but says she knows how to keep you safe in her heart. Maybe I'm learning how to do that a little too.

Writing this has made me feel much better. I'm going to do it whenever I can. Especially when I have something special to tell you. Like about Aaron. (I'm going to _love_ having those conversations!)

I guess that's it for now.

"Good night, sweet prince.

Flights of angels sing thee to thy rest."

All the love I have,
Tika

PS. I hope you're impressed that I'm quoting Shakespeare. From Hamlet, no less. I guess I'm like my brother in choosing smart people to fall in love with!

❧ 36 ❧

IT'S ANOTHER ONE OF THOSE ALMOST-PERFECT SUMMER days. Except it's almost not summer anymore. Summer's about to be a memory. School starts in two weeks and three days. After dinner I convinced Mama and Dad to make an ice cream run with me. "Ice cream weather will be disappearing soon, you know."

Bibi laughed. "Leah, ice cream weather thrives in this home even during blizzards. Just make sure you pick up a pint of butter pecan for me."

Mama and Dad and I have walked over to Harper Court to get cones or shakes. We only remember after we get here that the ice cream shop has moved.

Just like the benches.

Dad stops at the edge of the sloping part of the ground. Where one of the chess benches used to be. When Dad looks down at the spot, I wonder if in his mind he's seeing the long gray slab that had a chessboard etched in the middle. And Luce. Is he seeing Luce sitting on that bench, doing what he loved more than just about anything else in the world?

Luce would make a beeline for this place whenever he could. After he got off work from his summer job and sometimes even before he went. Besides going over to see Mahri, coming here was one of the first things he did as soon as he got home from school on vacation—even in the winter!

"There's snow on the ground, Luce. Nobody plays chess outside in the snow."

"'Nobody' is too big a word to use for chess players, Dad. Somebody will be at the court, looking for a good match. The snow is just on the ground."

Every single chess bench is gone now. I watch Dad look at all the empty places where the benches used to be and can't think of anything to say. So I just rub my hand down Dad's back. He nods his head and smiles. Mama watches the two of us and smiles, too.

The first time he saw the benches gone and heard why, Dad stormed into the little restaurant on the ground level of the courtyard, went up to the owner-cook, and got right in his face. Mama was with him and told Bibi and me about it.

"Simon was so mad. You should have seen him. *Heard*

him. He said, 'Mr. Hopper, I don't believe for a minute that the chess players caused a ruckus that interfered with your business. I think if they were guilty of anything, it was giving people an alternative to coming into this greasy spoon just to have something to do. As I recall, the choice had become picking up a cone or a shake and then standing around to watch a chess game. Business picked up considerably in the ice cream shop and practically disappeared here. Isn't that right, Mr. Hopper? And now that both the benches and the ice cream shop have gone, how's business?'"

"Well, after he said that, Simon looked around the empty dive and gave this almost evil laugh. 'Looks to me, Hopper, that your business has disappeared right along with everything else!'"

Imagining my soft-spoken Dad up in Mr. Hopper's face makes me almost laugh out loud every time I think about it. Dad, who's still just standing where the bench used to be, hears my little snort and turns around to look at me. "What?"

I don't want to get stuff started, so I say what had crossed my mind when we first got here and remembered that the ice cream shop had moved. "Ah . . . ah, I was just thinking that we should go on and walk to Kimbark. You know, where the ice cream shop is now. It's not too much farther."

"What do you say, Lexie?"

"Fine with me."

The three of us head out of the courtyard. Away from the empty greasy spoon. Away from the missing benches.

I end up walking between Mama and Dad. Mama links her arm through mine on one side and Dad catches my hand on the other.

"You know, Simon, being there—in the courtyard, just on this street—everything here is a reminder of our son."

Oh boy, it's gonna be waterworks time.

I look over at Mama. She's smiling.

"Yep. Proof that he was here."

I look over at Dad. He's smiling, too.

We come to the movie theater. It's been closed for almost a year now. The community council keeps saying it's going to reopen soon under new management. Nobody much believes that, but not because we don't want to. It's convenient having a theater within walking distance. Even if the movies are old by the time they get there.

"You're going to love this movie, Leah. It's beyond fantastic!"

I remember. Out loud.

"Luce brought me here to see *Crouching Tiger, Hidden Dragon*. I was *so* excited. Mostly because my big brother was actually taking me to the movies. Just me and him."

The words seem to hang in the air. Now that I've said them, I think I'm holding my breath. Then I know I am because a big breath comes out when Mama chuckles and stops in front of the entrance.

"I remember the first time I brought Luce here. It was for that special *Star Wars* revival. Remember, Simon? They were showing all three movies that had been made so far. Cliff had seen *Star Wars* and told Luce about it. Luce was so excited he almost couldn't make his little six-year-old body walk. He was practically jumping up and down before we could get across the street."

Mama turns to look across the street. Where she and Luce had probably stopped before crossing the street on their way to the theater. "Right over there . . ."

More words hang in the air. Then Mama turns back and laughs. *And* Dad. "I remember you telling me about that. How Luce actually stopped in his tracks when he looked up and saw that big title posted on the marquee."

"I can see him now." Mama raises her finger. Like she's tracing the missing title on the empty marquee. "'Mommy, Mommy! Can you believe it? I'm actually here. I'm actually going to see *Star Wars!*'"

Listening, I wonder if Mama's high voice is like Luce's was when he still called her "Mommy." The voice I probably tried to imitate when I called her the same thing.

"Did Luce like the movie as much as he was expecting to?"

"Did he ever! Simon, do you remember Yoda?"

To me Dad's laugh rings like music. "Do I ever. Leah, your brother had been so excited about seeing *Star Wars* that I stopped on my way home that evening to hunt down one of those action figures for him. I had my eye out for Darth Vader. That would have been *my* choice, so I figured it would be his. All I could find was Yoda, but I got it, thinking it would be better than nothing."

"Simon handed Luce that Yoda figure, and it was like he had handed Luce the world." Mama's little smile is sad but real.

"I'll remember it forever." Dad puts his arm around my shoulders. "Can you picture this? For months your brother absolutely refused to go to sleep unless his Yoda was tucked in safely beside him."

I rest my head against Dad's arm and imagine it. Wise, cool Yoda. Yoda and Luce snuggled up together.

While we keep down the street, more family pictures fill my head.

The four of us walking home from Café Bono one night and Luce stopping to lay something carefully on top of the pile of trash in one of the open trash bins at the corner.

"It's bread. I took all I could grab from the restaurant. Maybe a homeless person will see that it's clean and take it. . . ."

Luce begging Mama to stop at the health food store to get

some of the special eggs from uncaged chickens so he could crack one over the food in Mr. Jen's dish.

"That's what they did for the newborn kittens at camp, Ma. And they loved it. Eggs make their coats so shiny!"

All of us almost passed out from laughing at Mr. Jen that day. The way he jumped back from his dish when he saw that yellow yolk eye staring up at him from his food dish. He looked at us like we had lost their minds, trying to feed him that.

Thinking about it now, I giggle.

Mama and Dad look at me, both speaking at the same time. "What?"

The words come out automatically. I don't even *think* about trying to stop them. "I was just remembering something. You know, thinking about Luce."

We're almost at the ice cream shop. It's not too crowded so we walk faster to get inside before more people pile in. I decide that after we get what we want and are on the way home, I'll remind Mama and Dad of the fresh egg and Mr. Jen story.

Another Luce treasure we will always be able to share.

Our Luce.

For Allen,

MY ABSOLUTE BEST GIFT